CAMERA

Eva-Marie Liffner

CAMERA

Translated from the Swedish by
Anna Paterson

The Harvill Press
London

Published by The Harvill Press 2003

2 4 6 8 10 9 7 5 3 1

Originally published with the title *Camera* by Bokförlaget Natur och Kultur,
Stockholm, 2001

First published in Great Britain in 2003 by
The Harvill Press
Random House, 20 Vauxhall Bridge Road,
London SW1V 2SA

Random House Australia (Pty) Limited
20 Alfred Street, Milsons Point, Sydney,
New South Wales 2061, Australia

Random House New Zealand Limited
18 Poland Road, Glenfield,
Auckland 10, New Zealand

Random House South Africa (Pty) Limited
Endulini, 5A Jubilee Road, Parktown 2193, South Africa

The Random House Group Limited Reg. No. 954009
www.randomhouse.co.uk/harvill

A CIP catalogue record for this book
is available from the British Library

This work has been published with the financial assistance of the Swedish Institute

ISBN 1 843 43022 3

Papers used by Random House are natural,
recyclable products made from wood grown in sustainable forests;
the manufacturing processes conform to the environmental
regulations of the country of origin

Designed and typeset in Berkeley Old Style and Cochin by
Palimpsest Book Production Limited, Polmont, Stirlingshire
Printed and bound in Great Britain by
Biddles Ltd, Guildford and King's Lynn

Contents

camera [*Latin* = vault, arched chamber]. *See also*:

i. *Camera Lucida* or "light chamber", also *Camera Clara*. [*Physics*] An apparatus invented by W. Wollaston in 1809, which in a manner similar to the *Camera Obscura* (cf. below) serves to project onto a sheet of paper an image of an object such as a landscape, a face, et cetera, so that it can be drawn with greater ease.

ii. *Camera Obscura* or "dark chamber". [*Physics*] An optical instrument consisting of a wooden box, the inside of which has been blackened, with a convergent lens (or a combination of lenses with a convergent effect) mounted in its anterior wall. A screw fitting enables the user to gradually move the lens or lens assembly. The posterior wall of the box is equipped with a ground-glass sheet that can be advanced towards or removed further away from the lens at will. Rays of light travelling from a common origin and incident to the lens will be diffracted by it so as to converge, thus forming within the darkened space an upside-down image of objects in front of that lens, such as a candle, a face, et cetera. If the position of the ground-glass sheet is then suitably adjusted relative to the lens, the image will be captured on it.

Nordic Family Encyclopaedia (1905)

Prelude: January 1887

ONE WINTER NIGHT in 1887, Mme Helena Petrovna Blavatsky had a strange dream.

Before I go on to describe this weird dream in detail, I must provide some clues to the subject of my story – a few discreet signposts and beacons, as it were. It begins with a disappearance that may have taken the form of death – a most enigmatic possibility. The missing person became absent from the physical present and from all memory. Arguably, "being present" in the physical or mental sense is only one aspect of an entire phenomenon. For as long as a human being exists in memory, he or she must surely also exist in a spiritual way, be it as a thought, a soul, a ghost, an angel or anything else. Certain angles of observation will reveal the truth by allowing clusters of remembered moments, words or images to coalesce into a coherent pattern. New, unexpected truths might indeed be seen when the patterns are captured and studied. In this story, my intention is to recreate a group of human beings. A modest ambition!

Mme Blavatsky was dreaming, surrounded by the great sleeping, creaking house at Lansdowne Road. The mid-January night was freezing, and poor-quality brown coal from Silesia was burning in the stove. Its unreliable, feeble heat did little to warm the air. Madame, who had brought numerous woollen blankets and fur wraps to London from Russia, had piled her bed high with these treasures. The big bed resembled a massive Russian sledge ready to travel huge distances across the steppes through blizzards. Mme Helena slept fitfully, enveloped by the faintly acrid smell emanating from her nest of wool and skins.

This is what Madame's mind was showing her.

A steam-powered ferry was adrift in choppy, leaden water somewhere between Calais and Dover, waves whipping foam against the saloon windows. The saloon was empty apart from a group of Russian emigrants, most of them trying to keep their spirits up with the help of inferior vodka and songs from home. Mme Helena had chosen to suffer in silence. Her swollen legs felt unusually painful, and her ears were tormented by the piercing noise of the wind, which sounded to her like the sobbing of souls lost in Hell. Swallowing hard, she tried to distract herself by imagining her arrival in London. A great city! Also one in which she already had many valuable contacts. Her connections would allow her access to important people. The sour taste of vomit kept creeping up her throat. She gazed down at her neat black boots. The leather looked the way her feet felt, swollen enough to split open. She moaned.

A man she didn't know touched her elbow gently. A seedy, humble little man, that much she sensed straight away. His coat was cheap, and goodness – he was actually wearing greasy fingerless gloves like those worn by common fishwives at market-stalls in Minsk. When he leaned towards her, she saw only the gleaming, blue-tinted glass in the spectacles that were slipping down his nose.

"Madame, would you care to have your portrait taken?"

Apparently, the man was a photographer trying his sales pitch on her. Perhaps she was the only one in the group who appeared wealthy enough to pay him. He was offering her this novelty, a photographic portrait. In Paris, she had seen such images on *cartes de visite*. A truly elegant and innovative concept – in fact, potentially an excellent idea. She nodded graciously to the photographer, fingering the shawl covering her head.

Now the dream was taking her deep inside the ship. Mme Helena was looking for her cabin and following meandering dark passages that invariably opened onto the starlit night. The bowels of the vessel consisted of endless box-like compartments with tall, narrow doors. Finally, she opened a door at random and stepped across the threshold.

Once inside, the ship's movements seemed less abrupt. The room was empty except for a cat sleeping peacefully on the brown blanket covering the bunk. As Madame watched it, the cat changed shape and became a child. Its small body was a curious shade of blue and quite rigid, shifting stiffly about as the ship rolled. Suddenly, the child's eyes swivelled towards Mme Helena, and the chilly face opened into a scream, its mouth a black hole.

She woke at that moment, hearing the coals crashing in the stove with a hot, crackling sound, and the groaning of the house like a ship's straining timbers. Later, she would remember nothing about her dream except the image of the photographer and the camera's eye.

H.P.B.

IN THE LATE autumn of 1887, a new magazine boldly entitled *Lucifer* began to circulate in London's spiritualist circles. Influential young men such as William Butler Yeats and George Bernard Shaw took an interest. People who mattered were intrigued, though quite a few had doubts about it. Of course, the person behind the magazine was a woman and, worse, a Russian. Mme Helena Petrovna Blavatsky was alleged to be an aristocratic lady descended from an ancient family with both Russian and German connections, but there were rumours that she was a swindler and an adventuress who had spent many years in America.

Whatever the truth may have been, London was buzzing with gossip about that Blavatsky woman and her *Lucifer*. Mrs Allingham was thinking of including Mme Blavatsky in one of her exquisite novels. The "Countess" – or whatever she was – arranged well-attended spiritualist meetings at her home. The Lodge, as it was called, was situated in a respectable part of north London. Interestingly, the two Keightley brothers participated in the production of the magazine and also in Madame's nocturnal sessions. This must have helped to reassure those who might have felt uneasy about the respectability of the entire enterprise. Indeed, Madame lived in one of the Keightleys' houses: 17, Lansdowne Road, a comfortable driving distance from Holland Park and a highly satisfactory address.

Rendezvous: April 1889

MR W. T. STEAD, journalist and editor of the *Pall Mall Gazette* and *Englishmen's Review*, signed a note, sealed it into an envelope and handed it to Frank, the newspaper office's errand boy.

It was one of the first warm days of April 1889, and Stead's window was open. His elegantly turned wooden armchair creaked as he leaned back, his narrow hands clasped over his pale grey waistcoat. Stead was looking forward to meeting attractive little Mrs Besant, in his view a really good-looking, feminine woman. On the few occasions when they had met, she had been demure and attentive – ever rarer feminine virtues, alas. Apparently, there was a Mr Besant and a child too, but kept well out of sight. Damned important for a woman to have some experience of these things, after all. She was intelligent and observant, journalistic traits that could no doubt be put to good use.

A portrait of W. T. Stead shows a gentleman with neatly trimmed blond hair and beard. His hair was combed with a side parting, and he liked dabbing a few drops of verbena onto his beard every morning, being rather vain about his looks. He was an able newspaperman and a man of vision. His current ambition was to use the brand new, largely untried technique of photography to fill his papers with pictures.

Mr Stead's intention was to have Mrs Besant consider the implications of Mme Blavatsky's book, *The Secret Doctrine*. It seemed a confused, rather pointless load of scribbles, requiring the concentration of a woman used to careful, slow unravelling and remaking. He had a vision, first of soft white hands creating precise little stitches and then of Mrs Besant's hair with its red glow suggesting a hint of temper. Piled on her head, its bulk surely implied that, once undone, it would be a mane reaching her buttocks. Her sad, grey eyes seemed constantly to entreat him to be gentle with her. The armchair creaked again. Stead smiled thoughtfully to himself as he clipped the end of a cigar with meticulous care. He used a tiny pair of silver tongs engraved with his monogram (item 172 in the *Titantic* collection). He lit a match and turned the aromatic leaves in the flame. As his mouth filled with the cool smoke, he could sense something else besides a sense of well-being. Perhaps a childish feeling of anticipation.

He would ask her to visit the Blavatsky woman at The Lodge, maybe even to arrange for him to join a seance or whatever they were called. He would try to get a photographer to come along as well. Spiritualism was so fashionable in London just then. There was hardly an aspiring hostess in Knightsbridge or Belgravia who didn't take this into account when arranging parties, at least setting a table aside for automatic writing or a crystal ball for predicting the future. Well, he would predict the future in his own way or, better still, create it through the management of stories and images.

*

Through a pocket of time, a carriage moved along Lansdowne Road. Large, heavy and painted pitch-black, it resembled a darkroom on wheels. The two horses, in no hurry, now and then shook their heads so that their tack jingled and creaked. Maybe they were fed up and dreaming of fresh grass growing on gently rolling hills, but then there is no telling what preoccupies a horse. Pulling the high, solidly built carriage with its coachman and three passengers up that slow, unforgiving incline was hard going, though.

Lansdowne Road is an undulating, tree-lined street linking the calm, discreetly elegant area of Holland Park with smoky, noisy Notting Hill. The past is somehow still present in Lansdowne Road. Tough, ancient trees, their bark like an Indian elephant's hide, shade the houses, their great canopies sighing in the wind. Their roots push through the tarmac as if trying to return the cityscape to a half-remembered state of wildness. Behind sober brick walls, the bay-windowed houses hide in large, lush gardens, the tall windows allowing muted greenish light to enter the high-ceilinged rooms. The impression is of lost time, slowly fading into obscurity but captured in the centre of the city, locked into the very walls of the houses and rings in the tree-trunks.

In the large gardens, spring was just arriving in a flurry of new leaves and fresh scents. Mrs Besant watched idly as the trees passed by the coach's dusty windows. The slightly melancholy and watchful look in her grey eyes might have led a casual observer to assume that this was a woman in need of male protection and support, but nothing could have been further from the truth. Annie Besant, born in 1847 of Irish parents, was a clear-headed lady with a steel backbone. During the journey, she had been considering the questions she would put to Mme Blavatsky and only responding vaguely to the conversation of her fellow passengers. Or rather, of one of them. Stead was finding her absent-mindedness rather off-putting. Trying to control himself, his talk tailed off, and he leaned back against the cushions, his mouth tightly shut in irritation.

The other passenger had in fact not uttered a single word and might not have been heeded if he had done. Herbert Burrows, the photographer, did not cut a dashing figure. He was sweating profusely in the mild spring heat, a large Bell & Howell box camera perched uncomfortably on his lap. Designed for studio use, it was only taken out when Burrows was available and would humbly accept the task of hauling it about. Plagued by a chemical cold, he blew his nose into a much-used handkerchief. Just then, the carriage stopped with a last loud creak outside a large detached house.

The long rectangle of the façade and the building's depth suggested spacious accommodation, evidence of a substantial annual income. As they walked towards the front door, closed despite the fact that their arrival had been carefully planned, Stead mumbled something to the effect that the owners certainly weren't short of the ready. Mrs Besant had to tell him that she had not heard what he said, making him repeat the bit about how every year the Keightley brothers were likely to have at least £20,000 coming in, not including their mining interests up north. It was then that the door was opened by their hostess.

Stead's first, disrespectful impression was of a fat, shrewd old woman, who could have been the witch in some fairy tale, cautiously popping her head in its grey shawl round the door to lure little children inside. Then he realised that he felt frightened.

Madame had answered the doorbell as if there were no servants. Stead and Annie Besant made their way gingerly down the dark hall, noting that the house appeared to be empty. Burrows slipped, weighed down by his heavy camera, but Mme Blavatsky took no notice as she progressed majestically ahead of them, avoiding the clutter of suitcases and boxes with skill. An alien, prickling smell, a bit like something rotting, hung over these objects. Stead saw Mrs Besant put a delicate handkerchief to her nose and for a moment envied her freedom to display feminine weakness. An open packing case with badly tanned furs tumbling out explained the odour. Nearby, a stuffed wild dog fixed them with a glassy stare.

Stead's unease grew. He disliked being followed by that idiot Burrows, who was behaving awkwardly and causing an unseemly racket with his absurd-looking kit. He wouldn't use that clown again.

Suddenly, Stead's boot hit something hard but also as thin as an eggshell. The impact was a loud one. The object turned out to be a small, obviously ancient wooden chest painted in fading colours. Mme Blavatsky's voice rose out of the shadows. She spoke softly, with a lilting Russian intonation.

"My little mummy chest. M. Stead – just a poor little old dried cat."

Then, much to his annoyance, she began to laugh. It was a rumbling, quacking sound that struck him as somehow unfeminine, even coarse. He was surprised to hear Mrs Besant join in. His vague dismay was turning into anger as Mme Blavatsky spoke again.

"Let's continue into the garden. Into the Light."

Stead, still feeling cross, followed the two women and the photographer. The women were talking to one another, but he could not hear what they were saying. The door at the far end of the hall presumably led to servants' quarters, since the walls on the far side were painted instead of being wallpapered. A set of numbered call bells confirmed this. The ground must have sloped away from the house, because the garden door was at the bottom of a short staircase. Just as they were about to leave the house, Stead heard what sounded like a small child crying. It was a thin but piercing wail, almost feral in its intensity, and again he felt his mind fill with fear. He rejected the notion of the crying child almost at once as being too fantastic, soothing himself with the thought that the eccentric Mme Blavatsky must be involved in philanthropic ventures, possibly caring for the homeless and for lost children. As he stepped outside, he forgot the episode entirely. The light so dazzled him that his eyes hurt.

He walked towards the lawn, gravel crunching underfoot. Burrows was trying to rig up his tripod there, gradually realising that it wouldn't work. The man was a complete fool. Stead swore aloud, and Mrs Besant looked at him wonderingly with her grey eyes. Disapproved, did she? Just another silly woman, after all.

*

Herbert Burrows sniffled loudly. His nose kept running because the developer he used gave off an acrid smell that made his eyes water. His studio, located in one of the lanes behind St Paul's Cathedral, was, despite its proximity to a more prosperous area, surrounded by shabby houses crowded together. The sun seldom shone into these airless streets, where little seemed to have changed since the Great Fire. The studio was cold and draughty, the air pungent with the smells of photographic processing, all of which combined to give Burrows an evil chronic cough. At least that was how he explained it to his wife, Beth, who was very poorly. Having long since stopped getting out of bed, she lay pale and sweaty, her head sunk into a pillow covered in spots of blood. Herbert looked after her and served her tea in the mornings.

He coughed again. An image emerged slowly on the photographic plate. Some of the exposures had come out really well. Two of them showed Mme Blavatsky, a massive, inescapable presence enthroned on a rickety-looking garden seat. Another was a close-up of her face. Mrs Besant was in one of the pictures, leaning her elbow lightly on the back of Madame's chair.

Stead wasn't present in any of them. Instead, his image was etched painfully into Herbert Burrows's mind. He could not forget the way Stead had lost his temper yesterday, trying to control the photo shoot, his behaviour offensive to an experienced professional. Still, it was good to recall how pleased that old Russian lady had been. Herbert Burrows sighed as he started the tricky transfer of the sensitive plates to the bath of fixative. In the bath, it almost looked as if the figures were moving. The process restored to Burrows the sense of calm and pride in his professional skill that helped to get him through the long days.

He was a master in his darkroom, creating exactly the images he wanted. One second longer in that bath and Mrs Besant's hesitant smile would have been wiped away, vanishing into the corrosive darkness of the chemicals' reactions. He relied on his collection of dark bottles with their contents of strange, strong-smelling fluids. This room, like an alchemist's workshop, contained his entire secret art, his *Arcanum*.

He thought of Beth again and reminded himself to try and find some smoked eel on his way home. Surely they could afford little treats like that? She said she didn't have any appetite, but was delighted every time he made an effort to tempt her.

When he finally had his pictures ready and mounted in wooden frames to dry, he felt like a new man. The persistent pressure in his chest seemed less troublesome, and, leaving his darkroom (locking the door behind him, he reminded himself again to oil the mechanism), he found himself whistling the refrain of the latest music hall hit.

"Daisy, Daisy! You're my heart's delight . . ."

In the street, a garishly made-up woman maintained her seemingly endless vigil by a lamp post. She flicked her skirts provocatively at Burrows as he strolled past. He whistled all the way home.

"Daisy, Daisy . . ."

A Memory

IN MY DREAM, I'm waking up slowly, resisting all the way. I'm rising inch by inch through green seawater shot through with sunlight and dancing bubbles. The sensation is almost pleasant, but frightening too, as if something is lurking down there. The threat makes me want to pull my feet up under me, away from the unknowable depths. From the darkness.

Then I really wake up, with a thumping, splitting headache. My mouth feels furry and tastes foul after too many relaxing drinks in a smoky bar. It takes me a few seconds to remember where I am, and why. I check the phosphorescent face of my alarm clock, glowing faintly in the darkness. It is 3 a.m., so the journey will last for many more hours.

*

The wake of the England ferry cuts a crisp, frothing line across the troubled grey waters of the North Sea. The ship travels above the mud of the northern European shelf, above blackened branches of sunken prehistoric forests, stirring up murky currents sucking in and out between the rusting steel plates of torn hulls, the only evidence of forgotten, but once serious, intentions and enterprises.

*

She looks so familiar, I think. Once more, I watch as she laughingly turns her head away, making me feel incurably, deeply hurt. The pain is not lessened by knowing that the memory doesn't belong to me as

I am now, but to someone else who is a complete stranger. This has been going on for many years now. The pain becomes particularly acute when I'm travelling, perhaps because being in transit brings its own kind of instability. Mostly, that sense of detachment is a good thing. It allows one to respond happily to strangers, pretend that one is someone different. Someone who is successful and still loved.

I turn on the overhead light to find my cigarettes. I prefer the black, bitter tobacco of a Russian brand a friend gets for me from Tallinn. Yes, I have some friends left even now, though all the rest have gone for ever. I suppose it's because we haven't met up for such a long time that I can hardly remember what they look like. People might reasonably think of me as being lonely, or so I assume. I don't really care one way or the other.

Drawn-out snores penetrate the thin wall of my cabin. Next door, a family is asleep: Mum, Dad and two little girls. Overweight Dad was compulsively checking out anybody female, Mum was dragging the girls around, and the girls looked pale and close to tears. For a while, I listen to the recurring sequence of sounds, ending with a scary, small, slurping noise when the air hits some mucus. When I've had enough, I get up, slip on jeans and a black T-shirt, drag my fingers through my tousled hair.

It's not that I dislike men. Mostly, I don't care one way or the other. It's different if they get in my way, of course. I do dislike orderly plans, though. On purpose, I store my notes in a messy way inside an old writing pad, which I cram into a leather briefcase of the kind people's dads carried about in the '60s. It's dirty brown with a knobbly pattern like a diseased liver, two outer pockets and a tin lock.

I usually record my dreams in detail, but this one is so frequent that I can't be bothered. Just another water dream, with the deep sea thrown in. Actually, the dream notes are on top of the pile, then the photographs I found when tidying the flat, and then the diary. In other words, I must admit to maintaining a kind of order within the disorder – but then, who's entirely consistent?

I'll come back to the diary later. I've always liked collage, images combined without any regard for obvious connections. The new juxta-positions create a story of their own, unfettered by letters and punc-tuation, and more like a film sequence or a spontaneous spoken narrative. In some way, collages remind me of maps that can be read upside down or sideways, because no way is the right one. You are free to structure the jumble, imposing your own beginnings and endings, your own breaks and points of emphasis. This is of course what life itself should be like, instead of a pre-paid journey with compulsory customs controls.

*

The engines' dull rumbling makes the hull vibrate. It sounds like a large beast that must not be disturbed in case it wakes and causes a rumpus. For a while, I listen for the scratchy, shaky noises of a break-down, but the engines chug on monotonously. In the distance, the water crashes regularly against the sides of the ship.

Then the snoring stops abruptly. Maybe the wife has finally had enough. I hope so.

*

I arrange the pictures on my bunk. Some are old studio photos in faded sepia tones. Carefully mounted on cardboard, they are remark-ably well preserved. Next I line up my own enlargements of films taken with my old Nikon. It has a 49-mm lens, and I used either +2 or +4 supplementary lenses. All of these pictures form a pattern, but not one based on chronology. I have only a vague idea of the order of events. Still, they suggest a landscape in time or, perhaps more precisely, a record of a period lasting about four years. This is the time during which the boy was away, but still alive – that much I'm sure of.

Jacob died in the autumn of 1988, exactly one month before his hundredth birthday. I had planned to go back home for that occa-sion, because I always liked the independent Jacob better than my family in Sweden. Instead, I ended up attending his funeral in the chapel of Gothenburg's Eastern Cemetery. It was a typical November day, overcast, raw and damp, and I hardly recognised any of my relatives. I wished that Jacob himself had been there to talk to.

It turned out that he had left everything he owned to me. His will was perfectly legal, but rather eccentric – written in capital letters with a pencil on the back of an old paper bag – and stated that I was to have his large flat in Frigga Street and all of its contents.

*

It is a spacious four-room flat on the first floor of a spare, functional apartment block from the '30s. It has a view of a video-hire place, a colourful group of shops selling motorbikes and biking kit, an old Jewish burial ground. There is a large railway marshalling yard next to the cemetery, the sidings running very close to the outermost row of tombstones. Beyond the yard, the grey, sooty mass of the Lion redoubt rears up, outlined against Gothenburg's grey, rain-laden skies. Frigga Street is always busy with heavy traffic rumbling past and leather-clad bikers roaring about, practising turns. The sheer weight of this constant activity unsettles the area. Its foundations rest on mud deposited by the River Göta, and at times the whole place trembles like an old-fashioned jelly on a cracked china plate.

*

Jacob was a collector of interesting things. Even so, it took eight years and a heart-breaking event in my life before I decided to confront my inheritance. The flat had to be cleared out once and for all. One July morning in 1996, I stepped from the hot, noisy city streets into the cool stone stairwell of 25A, Frigga Street. Of course, I had been there before to do some tidying and airing, but I had never touched Jacob's things. I sensed his presence in the flat, a feeling that it still belonged to him.

This seemed just as true on that day in July. Everything was covered in the fine, dense dust that settles evenly in places where no-one is moving about. Almost all of the furniture had been purchased in 1936, when the building had been brand new, heavy pieces made of light, highly polished beech with striking inlays of a stylised sunset and a figure of the huntress Diana with the wind in her hair. Normally anything but conservative, Jacob never bothered with buying new things. In the hall, the bronze statuette of a naked young man in all his phallic glory still confronted visitors. The artist had been one of Jacob's "very dear friends" and also someone who had shared many of his interests. We never spoke about these things. We understood each other perfectly.

The hall leads directly into the drawing room, which Jacob used as a library. He had rows and rows of books about birds (for instance, the Wright brothers' series of illustrated volumes) and maps showing migratory routes. His book collection also included poetry and every kind of writing about games. A small glass-fronted cupboard contained "rare items". When I was little, he would show me some of them and answer my fascinated questions for hours on end. He had a Paris-made pack of tarot cards from 1820 that had been used by Mme Blavatsky to tell fortunes, and another pack of playing cards, much worn, that once had belonged to the legendary gambler Henry "Doc" Holliday. Imperial Russia was said to be the source of an exquisite and thrilling miniature chess set carved from "the bones of Napoleon's soldiers, or so I'm told". Half-hidden away at the back of the room were shelves packed with books about religion, occultism and esoteric beliefs, since "everything to do with death tempts me, my dear, death and any kind of experiences associated with dying. Don't ask me why."

Two photographs were displayed on a shelf. One of them showed Jacob as a serious young man wearing a rather smart bowler hat, English-style, and shiny white starched collar "no better", as he put it, "than a noose". He often said that his excessive shyness prevented him from living life to the fullest. The other photo was from his eightieth birthday and much more relaxed. His face was thinner and of course much aged, but there was a hint of dandyism about his smart bow-tie in striped silk, and his eyes were bright and amused.

He had set one room aside as his study, and I was only rarely allowed into it. After returning to Sweden, Jacob had worked as a free-lance photographer for the *Gothenburg Trade and Merchant Marine*

Gazette, which by then had become a better class of broadsheet. The paper had its editorial offices and printing shop in the North Quarter, housed in an old brick building on the corner of Merchant and Tryggard streets. Jacob's working life there lasted for more than thirty years, ending only when the paper lost out badly to its rivals in the '70s.

He put his best pictures in rows on the walls. The blindingly sunny views of Spain and Greece came from his longer trips abroad as a correspondent. Others were taken in his home town, showing the docks and the wharves belonging to the shipping company Broström. There was quite a collection of snapshots from his travels, usually of other travellers, including many of the well-known passengers on the England boats run by Swedish Lloyd, the *Suecia* and the *Britannia*. In later years, he always carried a handy, lightweight Leica in order to take snapshots of people without being detected.

*

I soon got over my initial sense of unease about disturbing Jacob's things, and, once I had started, my reluctance was replaced by curiosity tinged with an irrational feeling of doing something forbidden. Maybe Jacob would have liked being the cause of all this agonising.

The cardboard box had been stowed away at the back of the large wardrobe in his bedroom, hidden behind lined-up, polished shoes, all with proper shoetrees, and a folding valet rack. Having brought along the necessaries, I made myself a pot of coffee, carried the cardboard box into the kitchen and tipped its contents onto the table there.

The roar of a motorbike was absorbed by the afternoon heat and replaced by the sound of a clarinet from somewhere down the road, probably the music shop called The Golden Brass. The tune was "Take the 'A' Train". The hook propping the kitchen window open made a grinding noise.

*

Buried among the papers and photographs in the box I encountered a boy utterly different from the man I had known. Gradually, I came to realise that I must reconfigure the model in my mind. He had been my teacher, my father-figure. Loved.

For his entire life, Jacob had chosen to be a loner, an outsider. How could I follow in his footsteps?

I stayed in the flat for hours, going through the papers and examining the photographs, at first using Jacob's own magnifying glass. Later, I went to find a pocket lens. He must have foreseen that I would find the box, because he had glued an old magazine cutting to the lid, annotating it in his rather formal hand: "From *Bonnier's Monthly Record*, November 1910, on *'Diverse Thoughts Concerning Secret Writing'* by J. P. R." The cutting dealt with different kinds of codes and ciphers, including an example taken from "the fantasy novel by Jules Verne entitled *Eight Hundred Miles along the River Amazon* . . . in which an exceptionally good variant on cipher writing is described as follows . . ." The rest was a relentlessly punctilious account of how to decode ten lines of jumbled letters. Jacob must have loved it, but I've always hated riddles and charades and crosswords – all games that have fixed solutions.

I got up and lit a cigarette, trying not to remember that Jacob had disapproved of smoking indoors.

"You're dead and gone, years ago," I said out loud. That made me feel better. It occurred to me that I could look in Jacob's books on the occult for the right words to keep demons at bay.

My coffee had cooled, and I poured it down the sink. I threw out a dried-up old dishcloth and tried to tighten the dripping tap. The sound of the drops was making my head ache. I switched the light on and closed the window to keep night creatures out. It was almost 10 p.m., and I felt hungry.

After making myself some sandwiches, I couldn't bear to be in the kitchen any more. I ate them in the library, scattering crumbs on the carpet and not giving a damn. Then I settled on the worn leather sofa to think. The dry hide gave off a smell of cologne.

I could not help feeling like a traitor. This secret between the two of us would be the last one, a posthumous conspiracy that was neither amusing nor exciting. Only unsavoury. True, a long time had passed. The events of 1905 – from my grandfather's and King Oscar II's day – were real to me only through the jerky movements of an old newsreel, crude and roughly made, whose lack of dexterity might be mistaken for innocence.

"I wonder how much he understood, how much he knew," I asked myself out loud.

I needed a drink. Among the dusty glasses in the drinks cupboard stood an opened bottle of Grönstedt's 3-Star brandy. I wiped a brandy balloon and poured myself a shot, gently agitating the dark golden liquid before swallowing the lot. The burning sensation as the powerful spirit went down made me feel more alert, and I tried to think more calmly.

What chance was there of finding out anything at all ninety years later, I wondered. Sipping a second brandy, I found myself looking at the picture on the wall opposite me. It was very familiar.

It was a late nineteenth-century English painting showing a coastal scene with women gathering seaweed into large willow baskets. The tidal pools lay clear and still, and far away the horizon had blurred into greyish blue haze. The tide must have been coming in; foaming waves were breaking against the shore, and the women were taking a moment to chat. The youngest of them was in the foreground, looking out over the sea with her hand raised and her mouth half open. You could smell the salt, hear the waves and the piercing screams of the seabirds, warning each other as they circled away from the tall white cliffs.

*

I woke in the middle of the night, curled up on the sofa and feeling stiff and cold in spite of the hot, stale air. For once, there was no traffic outside. I had actually arranged to stay the night with a friend who was preparing to leave for Bosnia on a job and was busy writing up his usual detailed synopsis before going.

"I need to know what I'm going to see," he would say.

It seemed pretty incomprehensible to me, but he is a superb

photographer and one of my oldest friends. I liked his total lack of imagination best of all. Even so, he always left the last item in his prep list open-ended. Ready for a postscript.

"Hey, you never know whether you'll come home again," he would say. Always "you", never "I".

It was too late to phone him now, but the idea of a synopsis or plan remained in my mind even when I had gone to bed properly, as it were, stretching out on the sofa with a blanket and pillow.

You need details to clarify the past, I thought. It can be turned into an image, manipulated and interpreted. The past cannot be undone, but it can be reassembled. A new picture is possible, precisely because so much time has passed.

With this thought came an odd sense of security and then sleep.

*

My camera is a room, a chamber filled with light and darkness. It is also my wonderfully sharp extra eye, always lucid, never clouded by tears. I have been working as a photographer for the last fifteen years, though never successfully enough to be given an exhibition of my own after experimenting with dipping my pictures in acid or whatever. Actually, I don't much care for that kind of stuff. Not at all. I want to document what I see, provide evidence of my surroundings. If nothing else, I am at least a professional in my field. I record little in writing except for the details of my dreams, because they are images of thoughts and so some kind of photos too.

*

The snoring begins again, and sleep is out of the question. Lighting another cigarette, I pace the cabin. Three steps one way, three steps back. The toilet smells too badly to be included in my tour. Last night, I spent hours drinking in the bar, because I couldn't bear not to. It isn't that I can't abstain, it's just that the cosiness of bars always gets to me. Somehow, you must have a good time socialising there, though this time the people I was with seemingly hadn't enjoyed themselves for at least a decade. As far as I could see, none of them even liked each other's company. Dried-up females with dull hair, talking together in voices made hoarse by screaming at their kids. Lost males frantically trying to recall what "having a great time" might have meant when they were young. The whole scene sucked, but I couldn't tear myself away from watching these nuclear-family members without any fucking core to their lives. Maybe they didn't realise that something important was missing.

It could be that their existence drives my interest in completing the jigsaw puzzles of the past. I'd like to understand the chain of events that made these people who they are.

I've saved the diary, of which I could make nothing at first. It is a collection of impenetrable number combinations with which I struggled, wondering about the significance of dates. A diary from 1905, a game played by a boy with secrets to keep as the nineteenth century turned into the twentieth. What was secret in 1905?

I tour the cabin once more, the long way round that includes the loo, where I glance at myself in the flatteringly gold-tinted mirror. I don't make a habit of looking at my reflection. Liking images is all very well, but I don't care for my own. A woman soon to be 40 years old – what's your line, baby? What would they have said in 1905, assuming they mentioned such things at all? "Dyke" was surely improper. I could point out that I've had many deep relationships with women. Odder things have been heard of. I pull my lips back and show my teeth to the mirror. Pointy canines. All in all quite a decent set, despite the cigarette stains. I ought to stop smoking and drinking and falling in love with the wrong people. Maybe stop living – full stop.

I deciphered the boy's diary in the end, nosily reading his secrets over his shoulder, and now I'm about to retrace his life in order to get away from my own. Follow footsteps that were made ninety years ago, which must seem a meaningless task to anyone but me.

I suddenly feel desperately thirsty. Mineral water dribbles down my T-shirt as I drink straight from the bottle.

Breaking the code wasn't that hard, once I got going. Or to be precise, once I'd found the key. The boy had created a disc that turned. The figures making up 1905 recurred round the edge of the circle, assigned to letters of the alphabet: A = 1, B = 9 and so on. The number in front of each letter indicated how many steps to shift along the disc, as in old-fashioned party games. To interpret the sentences, one had to read in reverse, as if time was being turned back in irregular increments – a notion that made perfect sense to me.

About Images

SITTING ON THE bed again, I start examining the photographs. All of them had been taken in a studio, twelve pictures of the same room in sequence, with different compositions and under different lighting conditions. Where images are concerned, I become careful bordering on pedantic.

Feeling cold in my damp T-shirt, I pull on my sweater, noting a big hole where one sleeve joins the body.

I like taking photos of objects, recording details on slow film like ISO 32 or maybe ISO 25, fine-grained images that can be magnified almost endlessly. It becomes possible to enter into the image and look for a particular view of one aspect of reality. It is as if that captured moment could be relived – or maybe not. I sometimes feel that things go on happening inside pictures. I don't mean the inevitable chemical decay, but the fact that the "depicted reality" is a world of its own, existing within its own time. Old photographs often hold secrets, and in their wealth of detail, their richness of light and shade, new truths can hide as well as be displayed. The trembling of the photographer is still there to be seen a hundred years later, but the scene the photographer saw continues to unfold in front of you. The image is a narrative that never ends. Wondering if they would change, I have sometimes returned to photographs to enlarge them.

In the beginning, the boy's photos were unclear, but they improved as he learned how to judge light, distance, composition, exposure. With time, he became a practitioner of an exact science that describes a precisely calibrated internal order. In his later pictures, there are things to investigate and compare.

*

Hours later, I'm plodding along the landing ramp. The racket is terrible. The steel plates are shifting, grinding against each other. Like an invading army, we roll our bags along, fibreglass shells on wheels like ball-bearings. In them is our personal survival kit for a week or two. Or, in my case, for an indeterminate time. A pale, sweating man keeps trying to overtake me, his luggage trolley banging against my heels again and again. In the end, I turn to ask what the fuck he thinks he's doing, but he slips back in the queue without saying anything. Sensible answers are rare these days.

Having decided to hire a car at Harwich – a much better option than sharing a train with all these people – I push through the crowds to the Hertz office. Finally breaking free, I light a celebratory cigarette there and then, and start on another fag on the way to the car. No-one bats an eyelid.

Storing my photographic gear carefully, I feel happy about being away from home.

*

It is bliss to be secluded in my little car, a metallic blue Escort with soft, gentle gear changes. I put in a tape of Van Morrison, noisily laid-back in "One Irish Rover".

In December 1905, the question of Home Rule for Ireland broke the back of A. J. Balfour's Tory government. To what extent did the Irish have a right to land and to at least limited independence? There were other potentially explosive issues, of course. One was the Russo-Japanese War, with Great Britain as the ally of Japan, and another the confrontation near Dogger Bank when British fishing trawlers were shot at by ships of the Russian Navy. What with one thing and another, a wave of violent anti-Russian feeling swept the country, which might have resulted in war but for some skilful manoeuvring by the Prime

—24—

Minister. He managed to dodge the demands for female emancipation as well, avoiding all debate with the leader of the Suffragettes, Emmeline Pankhurst. This was before emancipation had gained the support of the public, infuriated by the publication of photographs showing beaten-up, bleeding women protesters. Annie Besant was one of the leading Suffragettes, a tough-minded Irishwoman who argued for Home Rule as well as for making contraception available to the working classes.

So the great issues – property ownership, war, class, equality – were not all that different then. Who are the masters? Who has power? It would seem that for the best part of a century, we've got fucking nowhere.

*

The road passes through privately owned countryside, mostly protected by impenetrable hedges. Here and there are open meadows and fields on the slopes of low ridges with bare black trees along their crests. The remains of the Victorian railway network follows the road, cracked red-brick bridges across muddy rivers and flood plains. The land looks as if it is about to turn back into a swamp.

*

I am in no hurry to reach London and pull into a lay-by on the A120. I have to, because somehow I've activated an electronic switch that controls the seat-heater, and my seat is practically steaming. Besides, I am looking for a side road and soon find it, just before a small grey cluster of houses near Tendring.

The sun breaks through the clouds, and the spring light is clear and crisp when I stop by the roadside and take out my camera. Wanting more contrast, I add a tinted filter in front of my 35-mm lens. Away from the road, an old hump-backed bridge crosses the river. The heavy keystones still lock the arch with its mat of dead, dry grass, but though it once might have been a main road to the sea, it now connects to nothing at all. Only strips of darker soil at either side, picked out by the bright light, show where the roadway once was. Wheel-tracks invisible to the naked eye have a shadowy presence that will be stored on the film.

This is something I learned about when working with documents of various kinds. Often you learn things unexpectedly.

There is time for six exposures of the forgotten road to the bridge before it disappears as the sky clouds over again. I walk away slowly, the sodden ground sucking at my boots. High above me, a bird of prey rides the warm up-draughts, maybe a kestrel but I can't be sure. I haven't brought my binoculars. Then it screams, a high-pitched, solitary sound – *krriiiieeee* – and I see that it's a falcon scanning the ground for something edible and accessible to its sharp beak. Suddenly, it drops out of sight, as quickly as the wind itself.

I drive on without stopping, through Chelmsford, Epping, Walthamstow. Endless suburbs, graffiti-covered façades and small shops open round the clock. Take-away restaurants selling tandoori, pubs, betting shops and bingo halls. Dream merchants. Meeting places for people who live in cramped, chilly homes. But the worn, old high streets have their own dignity and serve as constant reminders of social injustice, barricades against the threat of forgetfulness. I see a big black woman in torn stockings walking down the street with the proud bearing of a queen. It seems to me that pretence doesn't cut any ice in these areas. Everybody's hand has been dealt already, and all people can do is play the game as best they can. Perhaps I'm being excessively cynical when I imagine that people who live here are happy to stay on, don't want to get away. Still, there is a precision about the class differences here that imparts a kind of clarity I cannot find back home. I like to imagine that as a consequence these people feel a kind of solidarity that our diffuse equality cannot support. Class consciousness is both a good and a bad thing. There is a strength in the idea of class that serves as an impetus to change. I might be quite wrong, of course. Maybe this is a community held together by desperation, waiting for the Flood to carry everything away.

*

The large silvery graffiti next to the entrance of Seven Sisters Tube station reads "BLOODY HELL CUNT". Underneath is some kind of sign, like a signature. It could be a badly drawn swastika.

*

A stretch of motorway is being rebuilt, and I get stuck in an endless traffic queue over a viaduct. Below, a gigantic man-made quarry disgorges gravel, sand and mud. Close to the reddish mounds of earth stands a cut-off, empty row of terraced houses looking like a lost railway carriage or partly dismantled Lego construction. The sun shines again, sharpening the shadows in the pit and making it look like an old, brilliantly detailed etching. Maybe a scene of Hell in which tormented souls are locked one by one into stinking, hot shells of tin and steel. Hunger gnaws at my insides, and I manage to extract a chocolate bar from a bag. It's almost 3 p.m., and I need a pee. All of this is oddly familiar. My powerlessness makes me angry. Bloody Hell Cunt.

*

Naturally, I end up getting lost despite trying to follow the map. The moment when the real street grid and its representation part company is when I begin looking for a block that I should recognise easily. I lived in London for five years, in a tatty two-roomed flat on the crest of Highgate Hill, patrolling the city with my Nikon. I took photographs of everything – fragments, moments, buildings. Always structural elements in a state of decay or about to be renovated or demolished.

During some of that time, I lived with N*.

I feel at home again once I've crossed the wide Kilburn High Road, driving past Queens Park and through the narrow network of streets in Kensal Green. Then I go on and on along Ladbroke Grove, just round the corner from Lansdowne Road.

*

I always explore alone. It is the only way I can work. Because no-one was with me then, returning does not feel so painful – I feel I can still breathe easily.

Now for 17, Lansdowne Road. Gupta was right, parking in the drive is no problem. Fragile spring greenery peeps above the garden wall, suggesting a large expanse behind it. Small yellow buds too, presumably forsythia. The house is a solid mass of blackened red bricks and cream-coloured paint-work, with two rows of tall Victorian windows at either side of the front door above the basement. Gupta turns out to be living in a damp basement flat. At the bottom of the steps, the air is sour with the smell of cat piss. The remains of a dead mouse have been trodden flat. Just tiny feet left and obscure innards. I feel a bit sick.

The sign on the door says "P. V. GUPTA" and, in smaller letters, "CONSULTANT". Once upon a time, this was the servants' entrance. The door is plain, painted an indeterminate dark colour green with algae, and with its window boarded up. Two garden chairs lean against the wall, their varnish flaking and exposing wood the colour of old bones. When I press the bell on the warped door frame, it doesn't so much ring as croak.

Just when I raise my hand to hammer on the door, it opens, and there is P. V. Gupta, a slightly built man easily a head shorter than I am. He's wearing a long, shiny silk dressing gown in a deep shade of maroon. Well, something like that – I'm no expert. His bald, brown head is shiny too, as if it has been oiled and polished. The bluish network of vessels at his temples makes him look fragile. He's like a small male doll.

"Ah, delighted," Gupta says. "Miss Hall, welcome . . . Miss Joanna Hall?"

"Johanna," I tell him, nodding but not offering him my hand. I don't want to become his best friend, just to stay in the house.

I go on to say that my luggage is in the car, but that I'd like to see the rooms before I move in. P. V. Gupta accepts this.

"No problem, Miss. Delighted. Please enter," he says, stepping to one side to let me into a long passage smelling less stale than I had feared it might. Gupta himself is surrounded by an aura of sandalwood and obscure food odours.

Walking ahead of him, I stumble on the first step at the far end of the passage. Gupta makes a concerned noise and turns on the light at an ancient switch. The light reveals the dirty-white wall and a set of call bells linked to a crumbling system of wires: "Drawing room", it says, "Library". Several of the signs have come off.

"The house is exceedingly old, but there are no funds for refurbishment," Gupta points out unnecessarily. "The Society doesn't . . ."

I can't be bothered to reply and continue up the steps and through an original, heavy oak door. It opens into a spacious hall, where the gentry had benefited from faded but authentic William Morris wallpaper. I recognise the pattern, "Blackthorn", printed at the beginning of the 1890s. A stained length of modern rush matting covers the floor. With a total lack of sensitivity, it was crudely fixed in place by nails hammered into the dark floorboards. A beautifully proportioned staircase sweeps upwards.

Gupta minces after me, talking all the time. I stop to look up into the stairwell. It runs through all three floors of the house, and daylight filters through a dirty glass dome at the top. The diffuse light creates a strange effect, like that of opening your eyes under water. A fat grey cat watches me from the nearest landing. Presumably, this is the hunter who left bits of his supper lying about.

Gupta starts walking ahead of me to show the way, after telling me that my rooms are on the top floor. As he climbs the stairs with his strutting gait, he keeps talking, more to himself than to me. We're both panting by the time we reach the third floor.

"Boxroom," Gupta puffs, pointing at a narrow door at the end of a corridor.

"Your rooms," he then says in a less flustered voice, this time pointing at a door to our left. Up here, the light is stronger, but still bluish due to the dome. The air is heavy and still. I'm longing for a cigarette, but decide to wait. The cat comes streaking up the stairs and settles down in front of the door to my rooms looking indifferent.

The house at 17, Lansdowne Road is one of the last important creations by the promising young architect Reginald Stanford Mortimer (1859–1903). It is a strikingly elegant and eclectic mixture of styles, blending equal proportions of *Regency, Arts & Crafts* and *Moorish* design. The young and curious R. S. Mortimer encountered the latter at an early stage. He was entranced by it during his travels in Egypt and above all in Morocco, where he stayed during most of the 1880s. Indeed, he fell ill with typhus there and died in the dirty, primitive coastal village of Bou Ismail, five miles east of Algiers.

The property at no. 17 was designed on commission from the Keightley brothers. The financial situation was at the time highly favourable. It meant that Mortimer was on the whole given a free hand to create both the exterior and the interior, a circumstance that explains to a large extent the originality of the house. The tenants who, with the blessing of the Keightley family, had the use of the house during the years immediately following (the property was completed in 1886) carried out several crucial changes contributing markedly to its present notable features. The tenants included members of the London Theosophical Society.

W.T.S.

(Cf. *The Architects' Yearbook* [1903], "Obituaries")

This yellowing cutting, untidily ripped from a long-defunct magazine, is crammed into an envelope that Gupta rather shyly hands me just before he leaves me in my rooms. It also contains a contract for a three-month tenancy made out to me, a map of central London (British Tourist Board, 1971) and two keys. One of the keys unlocks the basement door – "that's our usual way in" – and the other is a shiny new Yale key to the door protecting my two rooms.

I survey the very large room. Easily about 50 square yards, it is furnished with two sagging armchairs covered in once-blue velvet and pushed companionably close to an occasional table in dusty comfort in front of a chipped marble fireplace – "Please, Politely Do Not Light a Fire." There is a tall bookshelf and also a scratched dining table surrounded by four unmatched chairs. I note at once that the table will be a good place for spreading out my pictures. A worn carpet covers most of the floor.

The second room contains a bed with an old-fashioned, well-stuffed mattress and, tucked in one corner, a large wardrobe with a mirror on the door. The mirror has polished edges. The cat is lying on the bed, apparently asleep.

I settle into one of the armchairs and light a cigarette. My back is still sore after having dragged my suitcase and assorted carrier bags up three flights of stairs. I have visited the loo as well, checking out the lie of the land. It is spacious but windowless, and the bulb is easily unscrewed, which means that it will do as a provisional dark-room.

There I sit, watching the damp stains on the ceiling for almost an hour. The biggest stain is central and quite large, like a continental map with peninsulas and off-shore groups of islands. Some of these are large and some small, like skerries. The long, sharp-toothed reefs are really cracks lifting the mealy plaster along their edges. As I let my eyes follow these lines, I think of what I should do and say next.

I begin by looking up the telephone number of the Howell & Peters Agency in one of my notebooks. During my last time in London, I worked for the agency off and on. Before dialling the number on my mobile, I pour myself a warming shot of duty-free whisky. It takes me some time to explain what I'm after, but finally I get through. I speak to a woman with a deep voice.

"Right, you want a Pictograph run – no problem, we have the program. I'd like to know a bit more about your photos because it's impossible to interpret *anything* without knowing what you're expecting to see. You know that. At least, not where documentary material is concerned. So, give us a theory and some details – time, place, context.

Then we can get serious about these images of yours." She draws breath for just long enough to let me mumble my agreement.

Howell & Peters is housed in one of the great concrete bunkers at St Katherine's Docks, but because it's late, we agree to meet in a pub called the Dickens Inn, a refurbished warehouse on the old dock. Her name is Kim Darken. She strolls in wearing a worn raincoat and a colourful fringed scarf round her neck, tall and stunning in a careless, shabby way. She really doesn't give a damn. I like her at once.

Howell & Peters is a well-established photographic agency, one of the oldest in the business. Their picture archive is huge, starting with Roger Fenton's collodion negatives from the Crimean War and carrying on from there. It's possible to find references to practically everything, though not to a portrait of Jack the Ripper, nor to an image of the sticky signature in blood he left in an East End doorway – it had been washed off by the time the photographer arrived. That seems to be just about the only gap. H&P has been collaborating with Scotland Yard since about 1910, and during World War II an Army unit was drafted in to help shift the archive out of harm's way.

The H&P computer program for recording and sorting pictures is extremely sophisticated. With Pictograph, you are using innumerable reference points to move about inside a picture. Somehow, this makes the frozen image turn back into reality. With the greatest precision, Pictograph reads shadows, angles and light, renewing the spatial dimensions of the original scene. The past is reawakened as virtual reality.

I pull the photographs out of my briefcase and hand them to Kim.

"It's too soon to look at the pictures properly, and besides, the light in here is poor. It would be pointless for me to look at them now." Waving them away, she has a drink. Her eyes are limpid and green, like icy sea water.

"Instead, tell me – what's the story behind them?"

The Dream Makers

"**I** DON'T KNOW very much," I reply. "It's a bundle of photographs. Tell me what you see in them." She sounds calm and encouraging.

Pushing our empty glasses aside and checking that the tabletop is dry, I spread the pictures out in sequence. Pale evening light falls on the table from a nearby window.

"Look, they're all taken in the same room."

I point out some of the details, like the wide door frame in the background and the wall light with its bare bulb. Electric light presumably only featured in privileged homes of the time. The room looks like an attic; roughly planed beams are visible at the upper edge of some of the pictures. The light comes from above, possibly through a glazed section of the roof. The camera was fixed on a moving scene.

"These are young boys, aren't they?" By now, Kim is looking at the pictures as if she had forgotten what she'd said earlier.

I nod. Some of the boys look straight at the camera, but the images fail to capture their real feelings. They might have felt defiant, or just lost. There is a jumbled pile of blankets on what must have been a cold floor and a large black stove that probably never gave off any real warmth.

"Do you have more pictures? And where did you get hold of these?" Kim asks.

"Some of them were up for sale . . . and I knew the photographer . . ." I sound vague, which is unnecessary. "He was my uncle. And I want to know what he was doing there."

The pub is filling up with people and the din of their voices, so we decide to leave. It has become dark outside. We stop by some old winding gear on the dock. It's a still, chilly night, and the stars are brilliantly clear. Lights from the boats at anchor are reflected in the water. Each light-image is split, rocking gently and seeming to float on the dark surface. Many of the old vessels must be inhabited, judging by the glowing lanterns tied to their masts. I watch as a lean harbour cat moves across a deck with soundless caution, neatly avoiding some dead-looking potted plants and then disappearing down a hatch. The boat is painted green and her home port, back when she could still sail, was Whitby in Yorkshire.

*

I light another cigarette, determined to tell a brisk, coherent story this time if I can.

"My uncle, Jacob Hall, was a photographer – a really good one. His parents were English, but he was born in Gothenburg on Sweden's western coast in 1888. His father, James Hall, was a merchant with interests in timber and iron who had been tempted by the lucrative Scandinavian trade in the 1870s. For one thing, there were few knowledgeable people on the Swedish side of the business, so all James Hall had to do was carry on as usual. The fact that local landowners had no idea what their forests and iron ore were worth meant that merchants could buy cheap and sell dear on the export market. It didn't take long for James Hall to become quite wealthy.

"Jacob's mother, Agnes, was a frail, nervous woman. She was fond of drawing and produced paintings of her five children. After the death of her second child, she became a fanatical spiritualist and joined a circle of spirit-watchers who met regularly to hold seances. Not all of them had lost close relatives; some of them were simply terrified of the fact that the century was coming to an end. In order not to annoy their pious neighbours, they described their evenings together as prayer meetings. Gothenburg had a fair number of Free Churches by then. The leading congregation included the rather fierce followers of a preacher called Schartau, whose teachings were becoming influential among the urban middle class. Anti-Semitism may have been another cause for the spiritualists' discretion, because many members of Gothenburg's wealthy Jewish families were liberals and often interested in spiritualism. What with one thing and another, nobody cared to make the seances too public.

"By the 1890s, the Theosophists had established their mission in Sweden, and Agnes decided to join them. They allowed her to carry on believing in spirits, and stood by her, providing support and protection. James Hall also joined in an effort to remain close to his wife.

"Jacob was the youngest child and the one Agnes loved best."

*

I drop the cigarette butt, watching as the glow fades and then disappears into the darkness.

"Carry on," Kim says, huddling into herself to keep warm.

The old dock is silent, asleep as the night deepens. The water laps against the hulls, the anchor chains grind faintly, and the metal in the new masts makes ringing sounds. A slight wind stirs the tackle and ropes.

"Actually, don't tell me any more now," Kim says. "It's so fucking cold. Let's go to my place." She points at a white boat tied up at one of the jetties on the eastern side of the dock.

"It's called *The Mermaid*. I never take her out to sea. She's been here for three years." Kim grabs the cable to pull the boat closer to the jetty. She jumps on board, and I follow her cautiously.

Her home is a sailing boat, about 8 yards long, with a narrow but cosy cabin used alternately as a dining room, a sitting room and a study. After climbing down a steep ladder, Kim slams the hatch shut to banish the cold night air. I slip past a pantry with a two-ring electric cooker and microwave oven. The next space is surprisingly large and dominated by a polished wooden table and two benches with loose cushions. A desk just fits into one corner. In front of it stands an old-fashioned swivelling mahogany armchair, screwed to the floor, and on the wall behind it are pinned-up pictures. Some are by Robert Capa, naturally. As I examine a series of old war photos, Kim turns on the lamp over the desk.

"These are from the Russo-Japanese War, the first war to generate a lot of pictures for the daily papers. That's a picture of Jack London, who became a war correspondent in 1904. Two years earlier, he'd made a controversial reportage about the East End of London, called *People of the Abyss*. The dailies published half-tone reproductions of photos by London and people like Robert Dunn and Jimmy Hare. They all worked in appalling conditions. Jack London was really trying hard to find out all he could about the filthy wartime stories. The film companies got in on the act, too, sending their people out to record what was happening . . . it was the first *media* war. The technology was in place – photographic techniques, wireless telegraphy, transcontinental underwater cables, the lot. End of sermon."

She smiles. "I'll put the kettle on."

"Why do you like images of war?" I ask once we've got our mugs of tea. The boat pitches lightly in the swell. Together with the warmth of the cabin, the movement makes me feel relaxed, even drowsy.

"They have a kind of purity," she answers immediately. "The photos capture feelings like fear directly, without masking them. This is the furthest limit for documentary photography, it seems to me. Unusually, as in sports pictures, there's movement in the frame, but – unlike sports – the action is uncompromisingly serious. A game, but your life is on the line. Capa was killed in the end, shot."

"How can there be movement in pictures of death?" I mumble, putting down my mug. I understand what she means, though. The camera captures what's there, or what was just there. The life that was lost. And, of course, it's better that we see all the bloody, ghastly things going on, much better than if we're allowed to close our eyes and pretend that there's something splendid about them, as in all previous wars. Military action and human beings dying horribly in wars have been glorified for centuries.

But then, on the other hand, isn't it possible that we're getting used to the horrors? That the *image* becomes acceptable while the nightmarish reality is pushed out of mind? That we're being reduced to the status of voyeurs?

I have no answers. Kim doesn't answer my question, just waves her hand absent-mindedly.

"Tell me more about Jacob," she says. "Tell me more about the prodigal son."

*

"Agnes Hall died in the winter of 1904. Jacob was 16 years old then, almost a grown-up, and must have been wondering what to do with his life. What his work would be. His father hoped that his youngest son would join the family firm. Jacob was given a reprieve, however, because his father wanted the boy to get to know England better. It was a golden age, the Edwardian period, and James, like most people, assumed that London was the centre of the world. This was before the First World War, before the old self-confidence had been buried in the sucking mud of the trenches.

"Jacob travelled to London with his father's blessing. The boy had a few years to spend on his real interest, then regarded as an 'impossible fantasy' – he wanted to take photographs. His father intended to keep an eye on the boy through contacts in the London Theosophical Society.

"At this point in the story, there's a gap of about six years during which no-one seems to have known what Jacob was doing or even where he was staying. Maybe he was in London, maybe not.

"In 1906, James Hall suddenly died after a trying few years of poor trading. It was obvious from letters exchanged just before his death that he had been caught up in a conflict with the local Theosophists about money. Although his firm went into liquidation, the accounts balanced reasonably well. Taken together with the fact that he didn't leave a will, there seemed no need to search for Jacob. Felix, his elder brother by a year, was happy enough to split his father's belongings between his sister Sophie and himself. Felix was always a miserable character, prudish and paranoid.

"Jacob reappeared in 1911. To be precise, on Wednesday, March 29, Mr Jacob Hall boarded the White Star Lines steamship *Majestic* to sail from Southampton to New York. Felix received a card sent from on board ship that caused a certain amount of anxiety before he realised that Jacob didn't intend to return to Sweden.

"Jacob's first job in America was with a photographic agency in New York, but after a year or so he went to California to join the industry that had just become established there: silent film-making. He worked as a still photographer for a company called Vitagraph until 1920, taking pictures of now-forgotten stars like Clara Kimball Young and Rex Ingram. There are still stacks of old photos from that time in his Gothenburg flat. A lot of landscapes too, images from Yosemite Park and Muir Woods. Jacob stayed in Hollywood until 1935, working as a freelance. Then, suddenly and inexplicably, he returned to Gothenburg. He might have been in Europe for a while, maybe in France and Belgium in 1917 and 1918, but I've got no real evidence of that."

*

"So you're looking for the years between 1905 and 1911?" Kim asks.

"Yes." I get up, stiff and slow after sitting still for so long. It would be nice to stay on, but the small, round clock under the wall-mounted bookshelf tells me it's almost midnight.

"You see, the photographs I showed you earlier are the only clues I've found to Jacob's whereabouts in the early 1900s. Apart, that is, from some notes and sketches that will take me a long time to interpret. They're in code, and different bits have different keys. Jacob was keen for some things to stay secret, but he would never, ever destroy photographs."

Arrival: May 22, 1905

T HE RIVER WAS heavy and brown with sluggish mud suspended in it. When the silt-laden low tide swept out into the North Sea at Nores lighthouse, the cold sea-water appeared marbled with strange floating shapes. The islands of mire shifted slowly, sometimes merging like storm clouds in a darkening sky.

The boy sat on a large packing case, his shoulders hunched as if to fend off the raw air, and his legs drawn up under him. He looked a little like the birds he loved watching – a rook or a crow from some dark forest, shy of people and secretive. He was warming his hands round a mug of tea, brown like river mud. Staring at the shapes moving in the water, he was so absorbed that he did not notice that the pages of the black-covered notebook open in his lap were curling with damp.

The sun had been hiding stubbornly and the temperature falling, so it felt cold despite its almost being summer. Every morning, the stiff tarpaulins covering the deck looked a little like massive bowls filled with condensation that had settled during the night.

The ship was waiting for a signal of free passage upriver. Gravesend provided anchorage for unwieldy merchantmen from harbours all over the world. Ships gathered at the fortresses of Sheerness and Tilbury, and their foghorns called forlornly, sounding hollow in the thick air.

The boy observed the slow procession of black ironclad hulls moving almost gracefully, as if in a dance. Meanwhile, huge wings of tempered steel rotated beneath the surface, slashing the water and whipping up all kinds of waste and rotting vegetation that rose in a stream of bubbles. The boy became fascinated, going to the railing to smell the water as well as see it. The smell was no longer salty like that of the sea back home, but hard to define. It included the odour of machine oil and flaking lead paint and the heavy stink of things rotting in the sand and soil from the broad marshes. The sucking tidal waters stirred it all up constantly. It was as if time itself was in motion, forming sediments and then disrupting its own deep order.

*

The estuary flowed through a flat green and yellow landscape, marshes where sedges and gorse formed dense thickets along the waterways. After endless hard labour, enough ditches had been dug to drain what once had been swamps and so protect the great city further inland from flooding. Where the wetlands remained, the lights of distant towns and villages were reflected over the fens for miles, gleaming in puddles and pools like the fading lanterns of a hidden people.

The waters of the river soaked through the mud flats at Gravesend, running faster at Woolwich and flowing in great bends past Blackwell and the tumultuous East India Docks. By the time travellers reached the Royal Observatory at Greenwich, high on a green hill, they had almost arrived at their destination.

*

The best part of two days had passed since the ship had left Gothenburg harbour. A few hours after dawn, SS *Aldebaran* slowly drew in at one of the smaller sections of the quay at Millwall Dock. The dock was on a loop of the river just before it started another slow bend at Limehouse Reach, which was almost level with central London. The shipping lane went close to the Millwall Tap Brewery with its tart smells of hops and brewer's mash. The chief mate kept watch intently as the edge of the quay came closer. His voice was hoarse with fatigue, and the coarse blue cloth of his jacket was tight across his shoulders. His face became furious when the cook and the ship's boy came by hauling stinking buckets of slops. The ship was a new one, and the chief mate was only too aware that the representative for Bott & Co., the London agent for the Thule shipping company, was waiting in the crowd on the quay.

The passengers were all on the upper deck, chatting and pointing. The boy was being pushed about, but it didn't bother him because he could sense the city's teeming life. A pallid-looking gentleman lit a cigar, puffing energetically. The North Sea weather had been tough on the travellers, what with the brisk wind that had driven the sea into foaming crests during the entire crossing. Now they could all smell the chestnuts roasting over drums filled with glowing charcoal, their odour mingling with the stink of steaming horse droppings that piled up along the omnibus routes, and the soot and smoke from chimneys outlined against the sky like so many organ-pipes of cracked clay. Other scents came drifting on the breeze: juniper from spilt gin and softly aromatic tobacco, as likely as not harvested on the huge, sun-scorched fields of Louisiana.

People were calling out, shouting, abusing each other. A strongly built stevedore, a sweaty kerchief tied round his thick neck, stumbled as he reached out to catch the twisting end of a rope and was dangerously close to falling into the slippery gap between ship and quayside. He recovered his balance at the last minute, but couldn't stop swearing as he made the coarse rope fast round a bollard.

The boy kept taking deep breaths to convince himself that he had truly arrived. His task was to find the address of a man who ran a newspaper. The man's name was Stead. His office wasn't at some posh address but at the far end of Fleet Street, the end where the road rose slightly towards Ludgate Hill and St Paul's Cathedral.

*

At Fenchurch Street Station in Mark Lane, the boy switched from the railway to the Underground. He had a lot to carry – the heavy wooden box with the camera and his suitcase, hanging over his shoulder on a strap. All around him, smoke, roaring machinery and loud voices filled the air. The hordes of people hurrying ceaselessly through subterranean tunnels and over spindly viaducts of wrought iron made him feel helpless.

He got out at St Paul's and stopped for a moment, blinking in the grey daylight before pushing his way through the crowds. He checked the map in his *Guide to London* again. This must be Blackfriars Bridge, criss-crossed by railway tracks on spans high above the glittering river. After following New Bridge Street, he turned left at Ludgate Circus and started walking along the wide, noisy street called Fleet Street.

Nothing in his polite guidebook had prepared him for the chaotic business of city life. He stepped aside at the last minute to avoid being run over by a horse-drawn tram, its bell ringing out furiously to warn him. Fleet Street, he saw, was edged by uneven rows of mostly old, scruffy houses. The office of the *Pall Mall Gazette*, it turned out, was tucked into an even rougher-looking lane. He spotted two heavily made-up prostitutes just across the way. In spite of the early hour, they were already patrolling the spaces between the sooty marble pillars of St Bride's Church. Such thin frocks, cut away to expose their white shoulders despite the spring nights still being so chilly, and, worse still, they'd probably been sleeping close to where they were walking, somewhere in the narrow spaces next to the church. A police constable walked slowly by, and the women adopted an air of greater decorum. The boy was mesmerised, but then a high post office carriage passed by, blanking out the scene. Taking a deep breath, he turned in at the *Gazette*'s door and knocked. As the porter let him in, the sound of the church bell ringing out 8 a.m. followed him up the stairs.

*

When the boy stepped across the threshold, W. T. Stead was sitting with his back to his large desk, looking out of the window. The editor's head was silhouetted against the large, pale rectangle of light.

The office was square, spacious but poorly lit and panelled in dark wood. A tall chest occupied one corner, each of its innumerable narrow drawers neatly labelled in copperplate. The great man must have done his morning wash and brush-up in his office, as a basin full of soapy water and a damp towel, comb and pair of scissors had been left on a small table next to the chest of drawers. The heavy oak desk dominated the room, its front decorated with an inlaid panel showing two crossed torches. The paler wood used for the flames glowed in the dull light.

"So – you're young Jacob Hall from Sweden, and you want to become a photographer."

The sudden remark startled the boy. Stead revolved in his armchair, showing Jacob his profile, its lines emphasised by shadows. He resembled a marble bust of a Greek philosopher deep in thought, with a strong, aquiline nose, a well-groomed blond beard flecked with grey, and heavy lids half-lowered over large, bulging eyes. The careful pose was only slightly marred by a bit of soap sticking to one long earlobe. Stead rose with surprising briskness and went to greet his visitor, holding out his pale hand with its slender fingers. His handshake was weak and slightly moist.

"As you know, I wrote to your father saying that you were most welcome to join us here. Apart from the *Gazette*, there's the *Review* and, of course, dear old *Borderland*, my protégé. The Society is always concerned that there should be ecumenical exchanges between its branches. New blood, all that." Stead fell silent, but smiled encouragingly.

The boy cleared his throat.

"I brought my camera. It's rather old," he said, lifting up the worn wooden box.

"I'm sure it will be fine," Stead replied, fluttering his hands as if to distance himself from technicalities. "Burrows will look after you. I just wanted to welcome you properly."

Stead turned away, stroking his immaculate beard. Although the audience seemed to be over, he spoke to Jacob once more, apparently slightly embarrassed.

"As I was saying, Herbert Burrows will look after you and . . ." he said, speaking so quietly that Jacob could hardly hear him, ". . . you'll be photographing spirits."

High Summer, 1905

THAT SUMMER, HERBERT Burrows and Jacob Hall practised the basic skills of photography together in the dirty yard behind Burrows's studio. It was baking hot there, and Jacob was sweating heavily in his black waistcoat, his shirt sticking to his back and his hair forever falling into his eyes. Burrows was in lecturing mode, hammering in the rules about light levels, exposures and composition. There was a long row of privies in one corner, and neighbours leaving them would stop to watch before returning home. Lounging about, clutching the privy key, they stared, whistled, cracked jokes, struck poses and pulled faces. Jacob had a hard time concentrating on light, time and the black box.

Think of music, Burrows said. Think of the caressing notes of the first violin striking up in the music hall orchestra. Think of beautiful Miss Florrie Forde singing her solo number at Gatti's. You see, *everything* must fit together. This is a science of perfection.

Burrows spent a lot of time going to music halls. Jacob hadn't been to Gatti's, one of the entertainment venues housed under the railway arches at Charing Cross station. After the show, Burrows liked to stroll down to a riverside pub called The Black Friars, not far from his studio, and have a few pints. He told Jacob that Mrs Burrows, having suffered from a weak chest for many years, was so poorly that St Bartholomew's Hospital had accepted her as an in-patient. Since then, Burrows had rarely bothered to go home, crashing on the studio sofa at dawn instead. When the boy arrived in the morning, Burrows would be hung over and slow-witted with tiredness. It usually took him until noon to pull himself together enough to resume teaching the art of photography.

Burrows had once been to Sandringham to photograph Princess Alexandra. His portrait was a formal, stylish image of Her Royal Highness, accompanied by her sons Albert and Georgie, before her husband became King. Burrows enjoyed telling this anecdote, which included a special mention of Her Royal Highness's fragile beauty. He would blow his nose with a sound like a trumpet, and then cough into his handkerchief. All the kids hanging out in the yard loved that bit. They rated Burrows highly as entertainment and would imitate him enthusiastically, blowing their noses into their small filthy hands and pretending to photograph one another. Meanwhile, Jacob sweated in his waistcoat.

Burrows and Jacob were expecting a visit from Reverend Charles Leadbeater to inspect the studio. Jacob had met Leadbeater once before, on the Embankment late one evening when he had followed Burrows around the local pubs. The pastor had been busy with his nightly mission of finding whores and other poor sinners to whom he would offer guidance, inviting them to his ecumenical services. Once Leadbeater's tall, lugubrious figure had disappeared into the evening mist, Burrows had told Jacob a little about him, whispering as if he was afraid to be overheard.

"The pastor is a member of the Theosophical Society, one of its most powerful and charismatic leaders. A very valuable man, and that's the truth."

Jacob sensed that Burrows's choice of words went against his true thoughts and was left with the impression that they had in fact met somebody unpleasant. Burrows, at least – one-time photographer to Royalty – found the pastor unnerving enough to try not to think about him. That night, in fact, he drank more than usual, leaving Jacob to guide him gently back to the studio.

*

Charles Leadbeater was a tall man indeed, easily 6 foot 4 or 5 inches. His curly black beard made him look like a prophet. Jacob shook his pale, cold hand.

"The Swedish branch of the Society is doing well, I trust," Leadbeater said without seeming to expect an answer.

Jacob simply nodded.

How pale the pastor's face was, almost transparent, his skin colour shifting to blue under the eyes. He breathed heavily, moistening his lips with his tongue. Presumably, he felt very hot in his black coat. Jacob thought that most girls would envy the pastor his shiny, cherry-red lips, but that they looked odd on a grown man.

"A drink, Reverend?" Burrows proferred an earthenware jug of cider. "The iceman has just been, and it's nicely chilled."

The pastor nodded, and Jacob was sent to fetch a clean tin mug from the scullery. When he returned, Burrows was already in full flow, demonstrating his large camera. At first, Leadbeater listened, but then he started asking questions. Why, he wondered, was Burrows still using glass plates? Why had he not moved on to Eastman Kodak's new invention, the film roll? Though Burrows was surprised by this question, he responded politely.

"In my view, the most important issues are clarity, stability, composition and sensitivity to light. And the photographer's dignity. Respect for his professional skills, if you will. All of which speaks in favour of the old glass plates!" Burrows was quite excited now, sweating and waving his arms.

Jacob poured both men another cider, adding some ice water to Burrows's mug because he was becoming alarmingly red in the face.

*

Leadbeater settled into a chair, leaned back, closed his eyes and steepled his fingers.

"As you know, Mr Burrows, I have views concerning the progress of humanity through education. My vision is of practically unlimited scope."

Nodding, Burrows burped delicately behind his handkerchief.

"Indeed, I have a dream," the pastor continued. "A great dream of uniting the advances of science with our yearning for spiritual values.

Reuniting may be the better word, since I feel that the distinction presently made between spirit and matter is an inaccurate one."

He paused, watching Burrows intently for a moment before resuming his speech.

"My goal is to fuse body and soul – to make human beings *whole* again. Mr Burrows, with your skill and equipment you can help me document this process for posterity. Following the laws of scientific scrutiny, naturally. Regrettably, my experiments – which might be regarded as somewhat delicate – are sometimes misunderstood, especially by the young."

Burrows leaned as far back as he could, cleared his throat and swallowed a large mouthful of cider.

"My skills are . . . err . . . at your disposal, Reverend. Naturally. And my assistant's as well."

"Excellent." Leadbeater rose so energetically that he knocked his chair over, but he did not seem to notice. "As you know, Mrs Besant has been on a lecture tour in America. She returned yesterday and would be pleased to meet you . . . and young Jacob here, of course."

For the first time, Leadbeater's eyes focused on Jacob. They had a curious, shiny white ring round the iris. They could have belonged to an animal, maybe a bird, Jacob thought.

A large bird of prey.

*

It was July 28 and the hottest day of the year so far. The heat pressed down on the city, and the streets were covered in suffocating dust. After seven weeks without rain, the authorities had begun to consider water rationing.

The coachman on the Fox & Co. hire carriage reined in his horse on the slope outside 17, Lansdowne Road. The sun-baked wheels ground against the metal brake-shoes. The horse, steaming with sweat after the long trip through the city, snorted and shook its head, making the tack jingle.

The front of the house was covered in scaffolding, and workmen were clambering on the roof, removing slates near the roof-ridge. Jacob could hear them swearing and chatting. Having been sent some money from home, he had bought himself a white linen jacket and a sporty brimmed cap. He was sweating as he helped Burrows unload the camera equipment. It piled up on the pavement: the large lockable tripod, the Bell & Howell camera, a brand new Goerz-Anschütz camera with leather bellows, boxes of glass plates and bottles of chemicals.

The coachman stayed where he was, high up on his seat, reading the paper and commenting loudly on the latest news.

"Entente cordiale – that's a new one on me. Mind, it's just another mingin' treaty wi' the Frogs and the Japs. Means war, that does – mark my words. I'm too old for a' that malarkey and a good thing too. Bloody Balfour!" He spat angrily, and the horse seemed to signal his agreement by giving his reins another impatient shake.

Burrows pulled the door bell. After a while, the door was opened by a tiny, pasty-faced girl, not much over 4 feet tall, with a mane of frizzy blonde hair. She peeped shyly up at Burrows, as if unsure whether to look at him. Her luminous blue eyes seemed curiously old for her slight frame. Her pale, thin lips were pressed tightly together. Burrows smiled and laboriously fished a card out of his waistcoat pocket.

"Photographer Herbert Burrows and his assistant wish to call on Mrs Annie Besant. There, my dear, just give your mistress my card."

The girl nodded and then vanished soundlessly, like a wild creature whose presence is so fleeting that it seems unearthly.

The hall was badly lit, but from where Burrows and Jacob were standing they could see the tall dark panelling and the wide staircase with its curving handrail, elaborately carved in a pattern of trailing stems and leaves. A tapestry in deep colours hung from the banister on the first-floor landing. It depicted the Tree of Knowledge and the Snake, the dreaded tempter, opening his red maw and hissing. The Tree was heavy with fruit swollen with juice and lusciously shiny, like silk. Gazing at this scene, Burrows and Jacob shifted from one foot to the other, uncertain what to do next. The girl did not reappear.

Jacob had a creepy sensation of being watched. Burrows seemed nervous too, constantly blowing his nose into his handkerchief. After a while, he advanced a little further into the hall and placed his dusty hat on a fragile table, next to a small beaten-silver dish for visiting cards. Jacob put his cap in his pocket.

When Annie Besant finally appeared, her entrance was carefully staged. She flung open the double doors to the drawing room, stopping in the doorway for a moment as if to collect her thoughts. Despite the hot day, she was wearing a dove-grey dress with a white crocheted shawl over her rounded shoulders. She moved towards her visitors holding out both her hands. Beneath her now white hair, her face was reddened by the heat. She quickly pushed back a strand that had escaped from her chignon. Her eyes were surrounded by a network of fine wrinkles.

"It's so good of you to come. I'm so sorry to have kept you waiting, but I was in the garden, admiring my roses," she said. Her voice was surprisingly deep and melodious, with soft Irish R's rolling gently over her tongue. "You will know, Mr Burrows, of Mr Yeats's poetic expression – 'Red Rose, proud Rose, sad Rose of all my days!' – so beautiful," she went on. "Look, I've pricked myself on a thorn. And you must be Jacob." She held out her hand to him.

"Dora let me know that there were two of you. You must forgive her – she never speaks. Dear friends of mine in Dublin asked me to care for her. Her parents are gone, God knows where . . ." Her voice trailed off.

Burrows cleared his throat. "We have brought all the necessary equipment, so if you would allow us to set it up . . ."

"No need to hurry, Mr Burrows. Mr Stead and Pastor Leadbeater are waiting for us in the drawing room. Let's join them and find out how they feel we should proceed."

*

The French windows in the drawing room had been left open to the scents of a garden in high summer, but partly drawn heavy curtains blocked out the light. Stead was standing at the window looking at the garden. On the dark floorboards either side of him, the square window panes were outlined in sunlight. Leadbeater's tall, pale figure was folded onto a sofa. The two men had not been conversing, and a silence had settled on the room. A fat cat padded across the floor. Seeing the boy, it miaowed and rubbed itself against his legs.

"It has got to rain! The river hasn't been this low since 1895," Stead was muttering, apparently to himself. "You can see the mud banks even at high tide. The quays are mostly deserted, and the whole of the East End is like a pressure cooker."

The sun seemed to mock him, for the light in the room intensified. Silence fell again, broken by the eerie cries of a peacock in one of the large gardens along the road.

The newspapers were full of stories about disturbances in Russia and rumours about plans to topple the Tsar. The Russians had become impoverished as a result of the war against Japan, and there was talk of ceding Sachalin and Port Arthur. Stead, who read such major foreign papers as *Le Figaro* and *Berliner Tageblatt*, knew that the summer heat had produced feelings of agitation among the working classes in Paris and Berlin.

"It's a dangerous situation," he observed to himself. "Europe is another pressure cooker. To cap it all, the English Marxists have merged with the Fabian Society!"

Mrs Besant touched his arm gently. He whirled round, and his face became even gloomier when he saw Burrows.

*

The eye was made of dark glass, a small, dense globe embedded among the arsenic-soaked feathers. Drawing with his charcoal stick, he managed to catch a gleam in the eye's centre. This creature had been shot, drained of its lifeblood, eviscerated and mounted against a background landscape painted by Captain A. J. Fitzsimmons in 1891. It had once been a kestrel. Its coat was a shimmering play of light and dark before shading into the black of the long, softly curving tail feathers. A slender aviator's body. A grey hood over the deeply set eyes.

There were hundreds of small birds in the display cabinet behind him. Tits, pipits, waxwings, robins – all stiffly arranged on painted branches as if gathered for a mute dawn chorus. The sounds from the museum's vaulted spaces reached Jacob from a safe distance, voices like the fluttering wings of small birds. So many creatures, fish, mammals – an *Acrocephalus agricola* and a tiny lark from the Black Sea. Grey monsters from impossibly ancient eras had been lined up near the main entrance. There were huge lizards from the Jurassic and Triassic, bones and skeletons found in the loose, chalky soils of the Thames Valley. Time itself seemed to have been caught and dissected, suspended in yellowing formaldehyde in rows of glass jars. Because the processes of decay had been slowed, the objects were preserved. The trade-off was that their textures and colours, the very signals of life, were gradually disappearing.

*

A little girl, wearing a blue sailor's dress and a round straw hat, stopped to watch Jacob at work with his charcoal sticks and pencils. She noticed that he was writing the date and his initials in the lower right-hand corner: *J. H. August 6, 1905*.

"Are they really, truly dead?" she asked wonderingly, looking at all the birds in the cabinet.

Jacob nodded.

"But who killed them?" she asked.

Outside, in the drowsy Sunday peace, traffic was moving sluggishly in Cromwell Road, though it was briefly disturbed by a cluster of racing cyclists in sweaty, tight yellow jerseys. They chased each other down the sunny street with much rattling of changing gears. Standing on the museum steps, Jacob idly watched the competitors while pondering whether he should stay in the park or trundle home to tea in his Sussex Gardens lodgings. At the stroke of two, his pinched-faced landlady served up a dry bun, margarine, a spoonful of jam and a pot of tepid tea. Although this was included in the rent, he decided to find himself a shady corner in the park, some peaceful place where he could read the volume of A. E. Housman's poetry which he kept in his pocket.

A week had passed since the visit to Lansdowne Road. The studio in the attic there was almost complete, glass panes fitted precisely into the roof and a provisional darkroom set up in a walk-in cupboard. The space still smelled of resin from the new wood used to construct the workbenches and racks. Leadbeater was anxious to start his experiments before the autumn drew in and the nights became too dark. He would have liked to start immediately and restlessly supervised the work, often followed by the cat, who had taken a fancy to him.

The weather had turned even more oppressive, clammy and hot and, in the afternoons, heavy with storm clouds piling up against a leaden sky, distant thunder rumbling like cannon fire. But no rain fell, even when the sunlight went yellow like oxidised tin. The papers ran stories about awesome thunderstorms in the north, including one in which seven torn bodies were washed up during an exceptionally high tide along a Yorkshire beach. Their identity was unclear, though they may have been sailors drowned during the Russian attack on the trawlermen at Dogger Bank in 1904. One of the bodies was wearing the shredded remnants of a woollen sweater, its fabric discoloured and almost dissolved by the sea, its pattern of looped and knotted yarn still recognisable by the Yorkshirewomen.

*

Jacob reached Queen's Gate, crossed Kensington Gore and walked quickly towards the park through hordes of chattering Sunday strollers, sportily dressed cyclists and trundling carriages. He noticed three Guards officers in red uniform jackets standing on the steps of the Albert Memorial, laughing, chatting and smoking pipes. On the other side of the road, a small gang of boys was larking about. They kept climbing the fence outside the Royal Albert Hall until a porter chased them away. Once in the park, Jacob became aware of a military band playing a piece from Franz Léhar's new operetta *The Merry Widow*.

Suddenly, the wind came up, making the dry leaves rustle. There was a smell of rain on the air.

Dora

I'M WATCHING GUPTA across a 2-by-3-yard oak tabletop. The wood is like granite after several hundred years of slow, steady growth, maybe in one of the King's forests.

Gupta has just filled the kettle and settled down to wait for it to boil, his blue mug in his hand. He's bright and alert; the morning sun falls on his face as he waits attentively for my questions. The fat cat is sleeping heavily in a corner, just a ball of fur on a none-too-clean rolled-up rug. I heard him patrolling in the night, so presumably there are rats about.

We're sitting in the vast kitchen, as if marooned on a desert island. The walls are almost a yard thick and were once white-limed, but they have turned a dirty yellow from greasy fumes and coal smoke. Perhaps the sedimentary layers on these walls could be used to trace the dinners served in the house, the well-hung sides of beef, poultry roasted to perfection, caves of hot jam under crisp pudding crusts, steaming calves' sweetbreads and so on. Dark patches mean that damp has been seeping through the brick walls, but the windows provide good ventilation and plenty of light.

Gupta pours hot water over the tea leaves, and we settle down to share a plateful of McVitie's digestives.

*

Over the last few days, I've been wandering around the house, examining every room, passage and cupboard. The smoking room, on the first-floor landing, is the best remaining example of architect's style.

It is decorated in a Moorish manner, intact down to the furniture and the colourful William de Morgan tiles in a frame above the mantelpiece.

The attic is the only place I've failed to get into. The door is kept shut with a chain and a large, clumsy padlock.

*

"Mr Gupta, I understand that there was once a photographic studio in this house," I say. "Do you know anything about it?"

Gupta dunks a biscuit in his tea.

"In the attic, yes indeed," he says. "It was converted in 1905, at the insistence of Pastor Charles Leadbeater."

"Any chance of having a look at it?" I ask. I mustn't be pushy, I tell myself, or the whole thing will go wrong.

"I don't think . . . you see, we store things there," Gupta says, so concerned that he stops chewing his second biscuit. "You see, the Theosophical Society is planning to move back into this house. Their present location at Adam and Eve Mews is too small, far too small, for their office. The Society's contract is still valid. Indeed, all documentation with regard to this property is perfectly in order."

"My interest is purely a personal one," I assure him with what I hope is an engaging smile.

Forgetting all about the biscuits, Gupta opens his arms wide.

"I'm only the caretaker," he says. "I must approach my employers before I can assist you."

"Thank you, Mr Gupta. Another question. Have you ever heard of a girl called Dora Flaherty? I believe she lived in this house between 1905 and 1906. She came from Ireland, somewhere near Dublin, and helped round the house. She might have worked in this very kitchen."

The light seems to be troubling Mr Gupta, who has started blinking repeatedly. He swallows another mouthful of tea.

"If you'll permit me to say so, Miss Hall, history is not a subject that interests the Society much. They are unwilling to go back in time. It's the future that matters; they're keen on new members, new knowledge.

Still, I feel I can trust you – in here," he says, patting his jacket in the vicinity of his heart. "I appreciate that you are engaged in your historical research and shall take the responsibility for letting you into the attic. Not that there's anything there except a lot of what the English call rubbish."

He walks over to a small cabinet containing several rows of keys, many of them old and rusty, hanging on hooks with labels of damp-stained card saying things like "Larder" and "Cellar" and "Green-house" and "Conservatory". The shiny key to the attic padlock looks like a brash intruder in this old-fashioned setting.

"If you don't mind," Gupta says, "I'd rather not accompany you."

Sitting down again, he pours himself another mug of tea. By now, the sunshine has reached the kitchen table, and the cat is basking in its warmth.

*

I had found Dora Flaherty's name among Jacob's papers. I think he had tried to meet up with her in November 1918, when a ceasefire had finally been established and relatively free border crossings were possible again. But she had already died in the epidemic of Spanish flu.

Climbing the stairs, I think of her death at the age of 26. The death toll in Sweden in this epidemic was nine thousand people, and those who were most alive, people in their 20s, were also the most vulnerable. Death came typically after about a week, and the corpses had to be buried quickly to stop the contagion from spreading. Harbour towns like Weymouth were ravaged first of all.

I switch on a light just outside the attic door. The well-oiled lock opens smoothly, and I carefully wiggle the chain free. The door looks old, but is very solid. It has a lining that is more than 2 inches thick. Was the idea to keep any sounds from being heard in the house? The hinges grind when the door swings inwards. It stops halfway, caught on an old packing case, which turns out to be impossibly heavy when I try to shift it.

Gupta was right. The place is stuffed with things, though whether they are English rubbish or not I've no idea – old lamps, school benches, tables, stacked chairs, cases and boxes. I find another light switch just inside the door and stand there, taking in the scene. It would take me months to go through all this on my own, and I've no idea how long Gupta's goodwill might last.

Daylight would be streaming in through the large glazed area in the roof except for the fact that the glass is covered by layers of soot and dead leaves, which make it look faintly yellow. The room smells odd, acrid and stale at the same time. I trace the odour to a large basket full of what looks like furs, presumably collars, wraps and coats. The kind of thing you would have worn for trips in open carriages and early automobiles. I touch one, and the surface is chilly, a little damp, but surprisingly soft, as if alive. A small, pale grey moth appears out of nowhere and circles my hand.

The Archives

WHEN I RETURN the attic key, Gupta is still in a trusting mood. He promises, again placing a hand in the general area of his breast pocket, to take me to the Theosophy Society's office in Adam and Eve Mews.

"I'll be your character reference," he assures me. "You see, all the important papers are kept there."

I know that in 1906 Charles Leadbeater was already in America, which means that there must have been a break in his work at Lansdowne Road – whatever it was. Unless, of course, he stopped completely. Anyway, this gives me a timeframe within which to work. Gupta tells me that the Society's archive holds a wide range of records.

"The Society has always been prepared to answer queries, precisely because its activities have often been questioned. They have kept contracts of employment, bills and all sorts."

*

The morning is warm and sunny. I'm due to meet Kim in the afternoon for my first look at the computer version of Jacob's pictures, so I decide to take the Underground down to the river and walk the rest of the way to St Katherine's Dock. After getting out at Westminster, I set off through tunnels of semi-transparent plastic film, where people's contours are suggested as grey shadows behind the moving surface. They're rebuilding the Westminster bridgehead, as usual. I hurry across the busy road and escape into the relative peace of Victoria Embankment.

It is high tide, and the Thames flows sluggishly, swollen with light brown water and the heat. I used to climb down to the riverside on forbidden and long-forgotten embankment steps slippery and green with mud and the passage of time. As the river rises and falls, things get left behind. Sometimes, you find pieces of Victorian stoneware, golden brown and perhaps marked "Doulton & Sons", fragments of jars that once contained strong, bright yellow mustard or cream-coloured lard. Or there are fragments of broken clay pipes, the bowls worn smooth by the patient grinding of water against sand, or rusting lumps of metal that turn out to be – well, anything from elegantly worked sword hilts to simple door-handles. This morning, the tide is already too high for exploring; the water seeps gently through the deep cracks in the Embankment's blackened masonry, ultimately reaching the medieval riverbank and maybe even engorging resilient seeds from the glorious seventeenth-century gardens which reached all the way to the water's edge. Further out, the powerful current is toying with barnacle-covered barges with names like *Filey Bay* or *Wapping*, making them plunge and tug at their anchor chains.

Here and there are marked stones indicating "Exceptional Levels" of high and low tide. Neap tides, always weak, happen when the gravitational forces of sun and moon cancel each other out during the first and third quarters of the moon. I have read that in August 1905, after that summer's interminable drought, the neap tide was especially low, and the markers are so far down that they are hardly ever visible. Only in an unusually strong flood, when the sun's and the moon's forces work together, making the sluggish mud shift, can the 1905 markings be read once again.

*

A homeless man is sitting on a bench behind Cleopatra's Needle, several carrier bags piled at his sandal-clad feet. His stench hits me as I walk by. The feral odour makes me think of caged foxes or wild dogs. He seems outside time and age, maybe 30 years old, maybe 50. His thin, sharp-nosed face is lifted towards the sun and looks peaceful. The bench has clawed feet like a throne.

I wonder what happened to him that he should be sitting just there. Is he past caring about hygiene, or is he no longer aware that he is filthy? Maybe he has simply stopped bothering – maybe it's that easy to lose your aspiration to remain human. All this comes to me quickly, but then our eyes meet. There's no difference between us. I immediately feel guilty. He could be me.

*

I like walking when I can get into my stride, so that after a while a regular, unforced movement propels me forward. I always plan the shortest possible route through cities the way a hunter traverses the wilderness – economically and purposefully. I prefer to be left to my own devices and, whenever possible, take backstreets rather than main thoroughfares.

People are beginning to arrive in the Embankment Gardens with their packed lunches, but it's still too chilly for me to feel crowded. I overhear fragments of conversation as I pass by – chat about holidays, the ups and downs of the stock market, sex, betrayal, elements in people's lives. It is as if I were tuning a radio. Alien existences pass by me but fleetingly, as muffled sounds, which is all I want. I want to keep people at a distance, far enough away for me not to smell them, hear their stories or have to sympathise with their piteous expectations and peevish whingeing.

*

I arrive at St Katherine's Dock at 1.50 p.m., after ninety minutes of relaxed walking, stopping and looking at whatever caught my interest. I do this whether I have my camera with me or not. Today, I left it at home, but I've stored images in my head to use later.

I remember my friend who liked to plan ahead and who went to Bosnia. Maybe we could have communicated more effectively now, but it's too late. He was killed one summer two years ago. Someone had been careless or simply not got round to clearing that particular road, and some miles outside Banja Luka his Land-rover hit a landmine. In that instant, when the image of war became the reality of death, he ceased to be an observer. His film was blown to shreds, of course.

I try several numerical codes at the Howell & Peters entrance and finally slip inside behind some returning lunchers. I can't find stairs anywhere and take the lift down instead. Its shaft reaches far into the river-bed. During the Middle Ages, there was a hospice called St Katherine's on this site, and I wonder if the bodies of plague victims and lepers are buried in the sediments, together with life-giving amulets blessed by the saint herself.

*

Kim works three storeys underground or, rather, under the river. Down there, the building's outer shell is spiked with poles, like a cement hedgehog, to stop it from shifting on its foundations of London clay. Even so, I see long subsidence cracks in the walls.

Kim greets me, looking great in jeans and a washed-out man's shirt made of some kind of shimmering green material.

"I heard that you were coming." She opens a door for me. "Come in. I've scanned some of your photos, and the computer is working with the data. Oh, and this is Neil."

She waves in the direction of a table covered with networked computers and monitors where a slightly built man of my own age sits, staring intently at one of the screens. His head looks large, perhaps due to the mass of curly, bright red hair that contrasts with his milky white face. His eyes seem an unusually light blue, but that could be the fluorescent light. He looks at me briefly without speaking. Above his sparse, spiky beard, his mouth is small and tight-lipped. It occurs to me that the beard might be an attempt to hide his acne.

"Neil is Howell & Peters' librarian, an archival genius who can find references to practically every item in a picture. Let's go to the common room to talk while the computer program does its magic."

"Not a great conversationalist?" I ask, once Kim had closed the door behind us.

She giggles.

"He doesn't like women," she says. "Poor guy, he's got to work with me for hours on end. We're sampling the University of London picture collection, more or less at random, but chronologically. Just now, we're looking at the 1910s. Next come the frivolous '20s. I cannot imagine working with Neil McGowan on that particular stuff. His family in Ulster are very pious, straight-laced Protestants all. The scary thing is, if you look at him carefully he's a dead ringer for Swinburne in early years, and, of course, they don't come more depraved than that. You know, I sometimes wonder if the same people don't turn up again and again. Working with old photographs makes me think that there's a limit to the variations of human appearance. Maybe we do have doubles – multiples – over time." She shrugs and goes to make us mugs of instant coffee.

"I've got biscuits and half a sandwich left from lunch. Would you like something to eat?"

I say no thanks to the sandwich, but accept coffee and biscuits. The common room is little more than a white painted cubbyhole, austere as a cell with its shiny tubular steel table and chairs. The only other fixture is a kitchen counter.

Kim notices that my gaze has strayed to a deep crack in a corner.

"It's at least comforting that it hasn't grown any wider during the three years I've worked here," she says. "But I won't deny that it gives you all kinds of bad feelings, working 25 yards below flood level."

I smile vaguely.

"Look, I brought you this," I say, handing her Jacob's notebook. It is filled with names, places and dates, scribbled roughly as if he had been working in bad light. "I think he wrote most of this in Weymouth. It's all about a girl called Dora – well, at least her name turns up in the beginning, and I'm pretty sure it's not in code."

Weymouth: November 30, 1918

A T NOON, JUST past its highest point, the sun was still low. The wind was bitterly cold. Ahead was at least a four-hour drive to Weymouth. It was a longer journey than strictly necessary, but Jacob wanted to avoid having to cross London. He was driving a British-built open sports car, a 1907 Sunbeam, entirely unsuitable for the wintry climate. It didn't run that well either. He had been forced to stop twice since leaving Hendon airfield to top up water and oil.

He had been warned. Hendricks, the major who had lent him the car and the necessary clothing – a fur-lined jacket, a pair of driving gloves and a leather helmet with goggles – had been candid enough.

"No time to look after the old girl. Bloody war, don't you know? Drove brilliantly at Brooklands in 1909, though. Rated ever so well." He had added a generously sized spare can of petrol, stowed at the back with leather straps.

Although Jacob had only left the French airfield twelve hours before, it felt much longer. This was another world, of green woodland and tall hedges lining the roads, here and there permitting glimpses of fields and meadows divided by ancient drystone walls. The scenery had no connection with war-torn northern France and its bottomless mud and ghostly black tree-stumps. Only the cold sky and drifting clouds looked the same. Although death had visited this landscape too, the air was not contaminated by the stench of carelessly buried men and rotting horse cadavers fermenting in ditches.

The day before, Jacob had flown in an aeroplane for the first time in his life. The plane, a two-seater Sopwith Strutter, seemed to be on its last legs – this was surely its final journey across the Channel. The off-white canvas stretched over its framework was holed by machine-gun bullets in long, criss-crossing rows. The engine's coughing worried him too, but it soon began to turn over regularly. Jacob tried, and failed, to read the pilot's feelings from his body language. He remained immobile; even his head in a leather helmet was still.

Rather like Jacob himself, the plane had been called into military service as a photographic facility. It had flown surveillance sorties over enemy territory, recording the movement of army units. The plane was of course unheated, and by the time Jacob could hear the waves breaking against the English coast, he was frozen stiff. Once in the aerodrome canteen, it took several mugs of hot tea fortified with brandy before he thawed out.

Now he was exposed to that icy wind again. The soft hum of the car's four-cylinder engine would have been enjoyable if it hadn't been so bloody cold. Then suddenly, as if the sun had read his mind, warmth and light broke through the clouds and illuminated the grey country road. The only other travellers were occasional cycling farmers, pedalling stubbornly into the raw wind. At the end of the terrible war, there was no fuel available for non-military uses. When the road straightened out into long, desolate stretches, he pushed down on the accelerator, driving so fast that the gravel sprayed up under the hard tyres.

So many deaths, he thought. Taking even small risks brought a kind of relief.

*

With the help of an aerodrome telephonist, Jacob had phoned a Weymouth number and spoken to Dr Max Frobisher, who sounded tired and tense but agreed to meet Jacob later that afternoon.

"I remember Dora Flaherty very well" was all Frobisher would say on an open line.

The sun disappeared, turning the world grey again. The road went through villages where wooden crosses had been erected to commemorate all those fallen in the war. Most of the crosses stood at time-honoured meeting places. The endless autumn rains meant that they were spattered with mud and already looked part of the landscape even though the memories they evoked were still raw.

Now funeral bells were ringing in the villages yet again. Men bound for home, their waiting sweethearts and wives, the boys who had been too young to go to war, were falling ill with influenza and dying in their thousands. Dora had died back in August, according to Frobisher. The Devil's own time had not yet come to an end.

*

The air had filled with light by the time he was near the sea. He realised that reflections from the water's surface were diffusing sunbeams like a huge photographic plate.

Dr Frobisher's surgery was in a road near the harbour. He answered the door himself, a tall, lean man in his mid-50s or thereabouts. His thinning grey hair had left a reddening bald patch. He stroked it awkwardly with his brown, veined hand, as if sensing Jacob's eyes on it.

"I've had too much sun – I take the boat out to do some fishing as often as I can. Forgot my hat the other day. The fish help with household expenses, and I get a bit of peace and quiet. Not that I tell my fellow citizens, of course. My office is through the waiting room."

The comfortable office had a large window overlooking the harbour. A mahogany barometer hung on the wall next to the window, and next to that was Frobisher's 1895 medical diploma from Trinity College, Cambridge. The other walls were decorated with watercolours of Weymouth Bay.

"My wife paints," he explained.

"It's very good of you to see me," Jacob replied. "To go straight to the point, I want to find out more about Dora Flaherty. As I told you on the phone, I represent a trust in America, and I'm trying to trace some children fostered here a few years ago. Can you tell me anything at all about Dora? She came to Weymouth in 1907, I believe."

Frobisher nodded, but instead of answering at once, produced a bottle of whisky and two small glasses from a cupboard.

"I was Dora's doctor for almost two years."

He coughed and took a deep breath.

"I should tell you that I've got a lung problem. It becomes more noticeable when I'm tired. Gassed at Ypres. My wife keeps telling me I should stop smoking. Going to war was crazy; I was too old and a pacifist, but once it broke out in earnest I just had to help save as many lives as possible."

He poured two shots of whisky and handed Jacob a glass with a trembling hand. Some of the whisky splashed onto his guest's trousers, and he shook his head in apology.

"You look frozen and – if I may say so – unhappy. I insist on speaking my mind these days. We have so little time allotted to us. Now, to Dora. She was a most unusual patient for a small provincial practice like mine. She was an opium addict."

"How had that come about?" Jacob asked.

Frobisher waved Jacob to an armchair and sat down behind his desk. Producing a file of patient's notes, he started leafing through it, rooting in his pocket for his spectacle case. Carefully hooking his glasses round his ears, he began to read aloud.

"Here we go. 'Dora Flaherty. Registered end of November 1907.' Right around this time of year. She had been sleeping rough for some time before coming here. 'Severely undernourished. Marked addiction to narcotics.' That was the opium. Not hard to come by at the time. In fact, all kinds of quacks were selling tinctures and drops and what-have-yous that were laced with it. A sickly child like Dora had every chance of getting hooked."

He read on.

"'She suffers from constant thirst. Allegedly has terrible dreams. Consistently refuses to speak, although examination of her vocal cords and larynx revealed no physical obstacles to speaking. Alternately very agitated and practically catatonic for long periods, during which she shows no responses to the world around her.'"

Max Frobisher took off his glasses.

"Is there a medical term to describe her condition?" Jacob asked. He remembered the pale, insubstantial little girl who had disappeared among the shadows of 17 Lansdowne Road.

"The best way to describe it would be as shellshock. I've seen the condition in the trenches often enough. Dora Flaherty had found safety in some place deep inside herself. Outsiders, people around her, had become unreal, so they could no longer reach or harm her. This is quite a reasonable reaction to extreme circumstances." He coughed again.

The pause lasted for longer this time.

"We tried to get her off the poison as best we could. It was hard, especially in the beginning. She behaved like a trapped wild thing; she even bit one of us. The dependency overwhelmed her and made her lose all control. At one stage, my wife was keeping an eye on her round the clock – oh yes, Dora lived with us then. You see, there are only the two of us. My wife and I never had any children. I think it's true to say that we looked after Dora as if she was our own. After about six months, she seemed to improve. She had a very special aura, you know, paradoxically very calm, harmonious. Light, in some way, and especially so when her true personality began to come back. She refused to speak, though, as if language itself frightened her."

"Didn't you ever hear her speak?" Jacob asked.

"No – well, not at the time. In the summer of 1908, we allowed her out on walks on her own. She usually went down to the beach, drifting along for miles. Sometimes, she would get as far as Overcombe. She collected things and showed them to us, looking very pleased with herself, things like shells and driftwood and unusual stones. She was childlike in many ways. Maybe she needed to link up with herself at a much earlier stage in order to be able to progress. Do you see what I mean?"

Jacob nodded his agreement. He had eaten nothing that day, and the whisky was going straight to his head. His tongue felt dry and swollen. He wondered if he was febrile. Max Frobisher watched him for a while and then got up from his chair.

"I'll lock up here for the day. You're very welcome to join us for dinner. I'm sure you'd like to talk to my wife. Of the two of us, she's the one blessed with real intelligence. You know, there are times I think that's a uniquely feminine trait."

*

Their house, high up on a hill, had a view over the entire stretch of Weymouth Bay with Portland on the horizon, a white wall keeping out the western seas. The fishermen were returning home, the lights on their masts blinking as their boats were rocked by waves far out in the bay. The wind was rising. Max Frobisher had brought a paraffin lamp, and its light flickered over the narrow, sandy path. The wind made the frozen tufts of straggling grasses rustle and whisper. Frobisher was wheezing heavily. Now and then, he had to stop to catch his breath.

Then, behind a dune, the lights of the house – a haven in the gathering dusk. Alice Frobisher looked small next to her gangling husband. Her face was round and friendly, with bright brown eyes and dark hair cut short at the back following the fashion of the time. Jacob had read several furious articles on the subject of women with short hair in *The Times*.

Alice seemed totally unfazed by his arrival.

"Mr Hall, I'm so pleased that you could come. It's a shame that you should visit us at this time of the year. If only it were warmer, I could've shown you my garden – it was designed in the style of Gertrude Jekyll. It's too dark to see it from the windows now. I hope you don't mind vegetarian fare."

The sitting room was large but cosy, filled with books, magazines and seaside finds. Apart from the kitchen, where they ate, this room took up most of the ground floor. A large brass telescope mounted on a tripod stood in front of a window with a view of the sea. Next to it, a collection of shells and unusual pebbles – green, rose-coloured, some speckled like birds' eggs – was displayed on a small table. A large fruit bowl full of red apples stood on another, larger table. The apples gave off an acidic, oddly dull but fruity scent.

After dinner, they settled down in front of the fireplace with glasses of sherry.

"Fifty years old if it's a day." Frobisher seemed more relaxed now.

Jacob watched him roll one of the decorative stones between his large palms. It was black and smooth as silk after being polished by the sea.

"Your wife is a talented artist," Jacob said, looking round at the many pictures on the walls.

"I certainly think so," Frobisher replied, obviously very proud. "Look at that one, it shows our garden in all its glory!" he added, pointing at a small oil painting near the fireplace. Its colours were bright, mostly red poppies glowing in the firelight.

"Alice is very fond of the art of gardening too, but up here the wind from the sea never stops, and it seems to shrink everything, to twist plants out of shape. On the other hand, we like the seclusion and the view. We can see everything that happens down in the bay." He drew a deep breath. "So – we'd got as far as the summer of 1908, is that right?"

Jacob nodded.

"Dora's health had improved remarkably. The seaside walks may have been good for her. She suddenly seemed able to *see* us. She *looked* at us, as if she finally believed in our support for her – and as if she cared for us. We worked out that she must have been about 15, but she showed no signs of becoming a woman.

"In 1908, Annie Besant wrote to Alice. They had known each other ever since the 1890s, when Alice had taught in a reform school in the East End and Annie had been on the school board. I don't care what they say about that woman, I think she's truly good. At the time, she wasn't that involved with the Theosophists. We were all members of the Fabian Society. I remember it well. George Bernard Shaw was a member, and of course Sidney and Beatrice Webb. H. G. Wells too, who writes those visionary novels now.

"Anyway, this was when we realised that it had been Annie Besant who had sent Dora to us. Beatrice Webb had been the go-between. We had assumed that Dora was just another slum child. Mr Hall, are you familiar with the scandal that broke round Pastor Charles Leadbeater in 1906?"

Jacob admitted that he had heard about it.

"Our Dora had been involved in something that had happened about a year before that." Frobisher's face looked worn and anxious now. His wife came in and sat down on the sofa next to him. The room was silent apart from the whining of the night wind. A gust came down the chimney, stirring up a spray of sparks. Still no-one spoke, until Alice decided to resume the tale.

"Annie's letter was both a clarification and a confirmation of what we had come to suspect. What we had not known was that the place where it all happened had been Annie's house." She rose and began to pace up and down.

"Annie Besant admired Leadbeater. I have no idea how close they were, but she seemed utterly blind to his weaknesses and indulged him in everything.

"Apparently five children were involved in the scandal, all of them boys. Dora's younger brother, Tom Flaherty, was one of them. We don't know the details, but it seems Leadbeater carried out 'experiments' on the children, using opium to 'calm' them. He would begin with a speech, some kind of sermon, and – well, it must be said that Charles Leadbeater was a master of the Word. I remember listening to him once at the Workers' Educational Society in Hammersmith. He was a good speaker, but a demon from Hell." She sat down again, and Frobisher put his arm round her shoulders.

"We've tried to find out more, but Leadbeater was a skilled operator and knew how to cover his tracks. The boys' bodies were never found. They simply . . . vanished. Some of them had run away from apprenticeships at sea, so there was no-one to search for them. We know about Tom only because Annie had undertaken to care for him and Dora. The others never existed, somehow. Apparently, this was far from the first time the Reverend had picked up little boys."

Her voice was becoming weaker. Jacob had to strain to understand her.

"Annie would never tell us what she knew. I wrote her letters, but she only replied with assurances that she knew nothing, adding that we, and Dora above all, had to look to the future, as she herself had done. Her conscience must have tormented her, naturally, but to no avail. I cycled to the post office many times to phone her, but without success. And when Leadbeater returned to London, she accepted him back into the fold, saw to it that he was elected a member of the Theosophical Society. Did you know that? It's utterly shameful. Since then, I've not been in contact with her. These days, she spends a lot of time in India, at a place called Adyar, I believe. The war has made communication impossible. Thank God that's over and done with, anyway! I mean that, atheist though I am."

She tried unsuccessfully to smile. Frobisher filled his pipe, lighting it with a spill from the fire.

"We said nothing to Dora about all this, feeling that she'd been harmed enough. She was getting better, and by the spring of 1912 she was able to address us by name. She soon learned another name, Jack. Jack was a lad – well, a young man – who would come every day to help me in the garden. In the summer of 1913, we saw it in bloom for the first time. It was such a fine summer; the weather stayed still and warm forever. The garden was full of lovely things, lady's mantle, white valerian, poppies, columbines, marigolds. Jack picked wonderful bouquets for Dora, wordless declarations of love. Delight transformed her, but she remained shy and withdrawn.

"The assassination at Sarajevo took place the following summer. Then the war broke out. Jack was one of the first to be sent to France. Like thousands of other young men, he was killed at the Somme in 1916. It was November and raining heavily; bodies simply disappeared in the mud. It took time to find them, and then they were hard to identify. By the time we knew what had happened, Max had already been working at a field hospital in Flanders for a year. Even though he was gassed at Ypres, it was not so bad that they felt they had to send him home. Doctors were in short supply, especially people prepared to work close to the front. Months went by before I realised that Dora was taking opium again. She was stealing it from the surgery. We would go there together, you see, partly to keep an eye on things – but yes, I felt Max's presence there, I worried about him all the time and was often preoccupied.

"Once we had heard of Jack's death, Dora stopped speaking again. Her grief was terrible, and I suffered with her, but could not reach her. She had no way of sharing her feelings. I hoped that she'd pull through it, but after a while she became unnaturally calm, totally indifferent. She gave up walking on the beach and stayed in her room for hours on end, apparently sleeping most of the time. Then I checked the drugs cupboard, and of course some opium had gone missing.

"What can I say? I lacked the strength to stop her – or the conviction. I understood that she wanted to escape, to forget."

Alice buried her face in her hands, her entire body shaking. Frobisher pulled her close in an attempt to comfort her, and suddenly his large hands no longer looked clumsy. When she had calmed down a little, he refilled their sherry glasses and put more logs on the fire, the flames sparkling and hissing in the draught. Jacob's body tingled with warmth and alcohol.

"What happened then?" he asked. He had been taking notes on a small pad, mostly names, places and dates.

"I came back home in the spring of 1917," Max said, reaching for Alice's hand, "and it seemed that my wife had got Dora's addiction under control. Alice would measure out doses of opium, gradually reducing the quantity, and they would take long walks together on the beach every day. When Alice took the boat out to paint on Portland, she always took the girl with her. Then this summer, the influenza arrived with the warmer weather. There was nothing we could do."

*

They invited him to spend the night in Alice's studio, which had been Dora's room. It was small, with a sloping ceiling, but the window looked out over a wide expanse of sea, now hidden by the darkness. The studio was furnished with a bed, a table and a tall chest of drawers in dark mahogany. Half-finished paintings, mostly of the sea and of the garden, were stacked along the walls. An easel was pushed into a corner and, next to it, a box of sticky paint tubes with exotic-sounding labels like "King's Yellow" and "Green Earth". A large glass jar full of paintbrushes stood on the windowsill. The air was aromatic with oil paint and turpentine mixed with a faint seaside aura rising from the treasures Dora had found on the beach. There were shells and stones, limestone fossils like orthoceratites, and smooth driftwood shapes treated so roughly by the sea that in the end the very core of the wood was exposed, its grim rings and washed-out knots like blind eyes. It was as if the original idea of the tree had somehow been restated in these tiny fragments, each lifetime expressed in a series of finely drawn textures. Sitting on the edge of Dora's narrow bed, Jacob kept turning the pieces over.

Alice had told him about her small portrait of Dora, adding that the girl "was terrified of cameras and any kind of images, so I had to work without her noticing". In it, Dora was looking out to sea, her head half turned away. The portrait was of a silent, secretive creature, he thought. He recognised the light thin hair, but her body had become womanly. He opened the window and the harsh wind hit his face with an icy cold that almost hurt.

*

Frobisher woke him early the next morning. Jacob felt surprisingly rested. Alice was still sleeping, so the two men pottered about in the small kitchen. Later, they walked together along the steep path, watching the sea and the rising sun, a pale, cool yellow in the clear winter air. Portland looked like a huge iceberg. It was a wonderful morning. The wind had died down to a faint breeze that softly stirred the grasses and reeds. Seabirds circled high above the rocks, screaming gulls and terns white against the blue sky.

Jacob told Frobisher about his great interest in birds and about how ghostly he had found the silent mornings in France once the ceasefire had come into force. The guns had stopped, but so had the birds, and the world seemed tired out, maybe dead. Max interrupted him suddenly.

"There's something I didn't tell you yesterday."

They had stopped to admire the view over the bays at Weymouth and Lyme. The tall, crumbling chalk cliffs with their rich stores of fossils were monuments of an ancient past. Max filled his pipe with his back to the breeze.

"You see, I've never told Alice this. I was afraid that she wouldn't understand. It is relevant to the story, though. Especially to that monster Leadbeater and his disgusting intrigues. You and I will probably never meet again. So I feel . . . anyway, I recognise something in you, something I trust. It's as if I'd known you for a long time."

Jacob nodded. Frobisher drew on his pipe.

"The event I want to tell you about took place in 1916, just before Christmas. I had recently learned that Jack had been killed. It upset me deeply, even though I dealt with dying young men every working day. On that particular day, I was at the Arran front caring for men in such bad shape that they couldn't be transported to the field hospital." He paused.

"Go on," Jacob urged him.

"I wanted to be alone for a while," Frobisher continued, his voice harsh and slow. "Stupidly, I walked off on my own. Of course, I followed the trenches, but the Germans had taken some sections the night before, and I must have got into one of those by mistake. Suddenly, I was surrounded by the stench of death and heard rats screeching as they fought over cadavers. All I wanted was to get back among my own people. Then I came across a lone German soldier crouching in a shell-crater. I've no idea why he was on his own. Maybe he too had indulged a wish for solitude. Anyway, he was just a boy – maybe the same age as Jack.

"We stared at each other for maybe thirty seconds. His eyes looked intensely blue in the narrow beam of my torch. Then he lifted his rifle, ready to shoot.

"Now, I've always been a peaceable sort of chap. I had no idea of my own capacity for violence. But I leapt at him instantly, got my hands round his neck and squeezed. Hard – with all my strength. I remember a sense of amazement at how slender and fragile his neck was, like a child's. He died after a few minutes, kicking up a lot of mud. His hands were tearing, scratching at my uniform. He was staring into my eyes as he died. I watched him die.

"Somehow, I found my way back to the British section. I've never told anyone. I'm a doctor, and my job is to save lives, not take them."

Jacob put his hand gently on Frobisher's shoulder.

"What else could you have done? It was self-defence. In wartime. He would've killed you in whichever way he could."

Frobisher did not speak, but turned away almost brusquely to stare out over the sea. It took him time to get the words out, and his voice was reduced to a whisper.

"The truth is that I liked it. I enjoyed killing him. I remember that feeling too, as an intense awareness of being alive. Satisfaction that it was I who was going to live. Like an animal. No better than an animal."

He fell silent again, and they walked back down the hill.

*

Kim looks at me when she finishes reading the notes.

"Let's hand this over to Neil. He can phone or fax the Weymouth library in case there are names or other data you can't trace." Kim gets up and vanishes through the door.

My heart rate settles down. She makes me feel unsafe.

Not long afterwards, she calls me over.

"This is one of the first images in your series. In a way, it looks like an unplanned exposure, because the man is standing with his back to the camera. His coat is in close-up . . . look at that frame, it's around the area the computer is working with."

We're sitting in front of a big monitor watching the software pick over the data in a small square of the dark foreground shape that is the man's back. At first, I can't see anything that makes sense inside the frame, which seems to obscure, even distort, the original. Then it grows more distinct. I feel the man might turn round to face me any second.

His back is broad and muscular, that much is clear from the way the coat fits, its cloth pulled tight over his wide shoulders. His hair is quite long, dark but with thick greying strands, and looks a little unkempt. The image has become so detailed that it almost seems possible to distinguish individual coarse and slightly curly hairs on his scalp. Instinctively, I sit back in the chair. The coat has a stiff strap at the small of the back, held in place with two buttons as if it was a uniform jacket of some sort. An official's formal dress?

The man has placed one hand on his back, resting above his broad behind, in the classical pose suggesting deep thought. Even so, his stance seems more threatening than philosophical. The big body is somehow stilled in mid-movement, as if an attack is being held back momentarily. I think of a wild animal, stalking.

A boy is sitting in front of the man, at the edge of the frame. He is a thin little creature wrapped in a big blanket. He is looking up at the man, but his face is just a pale oval, half-outside the clear image. He must have moved backwards during the long exposure time, presumably lengthened by the poor light. It looks like night-time, and the circle of light stops behind the boy. Maybe this is just a trial shot?

"Have you noticed the bag he's put down on the floor?" Kim asks. "Look, there in the corner. A leather Gladstone bag or something, with metal handles."

Once more the software dictates a straight sweep across the image. The details become even clearer. Yes, it's a bag, and the fastening is undone, but we cannot alter the angle enough to see what's inside. The image is very sharp now, the shadows making every crevice in the worn leather stand out in relief.

"Could he be a doctor?" Neil asks. He is standing behind us. "It looks like a doctor's bag anyway, just the kind they used in the 1890s.

Even the poorest East End practitioner would have his name embossed in gold letters on the leather. Try getting a bit closer."

Kim touches the keys and zooms in on the bag. Now I can see individual scratches and cracks. It must have been an old bag even then. There is no lettering, or else the name has been carefully filed away; the surface is too worn to say for sure. The magnification reveals one new feature, a thin rope sticking up from the bag.

*

When Kim turns off the image, I immediately start rooting around to find my cigarettes, overtaken by a deep sense of unease. The computer has made me feel like a participant in whatever went on. The coffee in my stomach is as bitter as gall. I realise that Neil McGowan is watching me with his bleak eyes, and I put the cigarettes away again. He keeps one of his hands in front of his mouth a lot, presumably because he has got bad teeth. He gets up, potters about and, settling down at his desk, starts examining Jacob's notes carefully. Now and then, he sighs with satisfaction, sounding like a guitarist reaching the ultimate chords.

"French, this is – Gallimard, manufactured some time during the First World War," he says in his strangulated voice. "Poor paper, very high acid content."

"November 30, two weeks after the ceasefire," he goes on. "Never heard of the Frobishers . . . nor of Dora. Annie Besant, now – she's quite well known, as are the Webbs, of course . . . Fabian Society, soft social reformers . . ."

I hear him suck on his teeth, watch as he fingers his puny beard and then turns to look through a shelf of telephone directories. He extracts the volume for Dorset, which includes Poole, Bournemouth and Weymouth. Kim wanders over to me and puts her hand under my arm. Her fingers are surprisingly cold and feel stronger than I might have guessed.

"Come on, let's go up to the surface. Neil can be left on his own for a bit," she whispers in my ear.

From the eighth floor of the Howell & Peters building, you get a panoramic view of the river and Tower Hill, where the upper classes used to get their heads chopped off. Archaeologists are digging in the old moat below the Devereux Tower. Because it's a sunny day, they've pulled back the tarpaulins, and their tiny, muddy figures are exposed to observation. There's a photographer taking pictures to document the dig, sometimes crouching in the ditch to get a good close-up.

The whole eighth floor is some kind of exhibition space with display screens creating long galleries. Mounted copies of photographs from the great H&P archive cover the screens, and among them I spot images of the river. An 1843 calotype by William Henry Fox Talbot, taken though air laden with coal dust and illuminated by bright sunlight. The conditions blurred the detail in a line of shabby warehouses, their façades no wider than the houses of Dutch merchants. Above them, a rambling forest of chimney pipes is outlined against the sky, the pipes leaning this way and that from the central stack, like cider jugs piled on a rickety pub shelf. A hand-coloured collodion negative from 1857 by Roger Fenton shows red-coated soldiers in the Crimean War taking a break by the river. They are resting in the sunshine, near where the Victoria Embankment will be built some ten years later. On the opposite wall and in mega-magnification is a 1937 bromide print in jet black and shimmering silver entitled *Metropolis*, a shot of what was then the new Battersea Power Station by Noel Griggs.

"What are your plans?" Kim asks. "Will you go home once you've got answers to your questions?" She looks at me, her eyes narrowed against the unusually bright daylight.

"I'm not sure," I tell her. "I've inherited a flat back home, so I thought I might try it out, I mean, try living in the same place for at least a few years. I'm not sure I can cope with going to the same shops, meeting the same people on the stairs. Being recognised. At least, it used to frighten me very much, but maybe I've changed. Or 'back home' has changed enough for me not to feel I've got to hide. It's all so alien now."

I look closely at a Valentine Blanchard picture, a small photo from

1862. A carriage has pulled in at Temple Bar. Half-hidden in the sepia mist, vanishing out of time, other hire carriages are queuing at the gateway.

I have never revealed so much about myself to someone I didn't know. Fuck it, I'll regret this. Not yet, though. Not yet.

Kim nods, as if my response was perfectly sensible – maybe slightly paranoid but not unhealthy.

"All I want to do is sail *The Mermaid* to faraway places. No immediate plans, though. I can't afford it just now," she says, and makes a face. She too is watching the street scene, bending forward enough for me to feel her soft hair so close to my face that for a moment her nearness is like a touch. I breathe in, trying to concentrate on whether I find the sensation uncomfortable or not. I peer sideways at her profile, hoping she won't notice. Her features are irregular, not beautiful at all if analysed separately. Her nose is too big; a long, thin scar has drawn a white line through one of her dark eyebrows. Somehow, it makes her look quizzical, almost supercilious. Her determined mouth is too big as well, and her skin and lips are very pale.

She senses that I'm gazing at her and looks at me, but neither of us speaks. Is she raising her eyebrows, just a little?

"I must show you something," she says.

Accidentally bumping against each other as we turn, we leave the gallery.

*

The photographic archives are located below ground, away from dangerous and slowly destructive daylight. The section for central London, 1850–1950, is one floor down. That century generated enough pictures to fill miles of stacks. Each block of grey-painted steel shelving can be manoeuvred by little wheels, and the top shelves, at least 15 feet high, can only be reached by metal ladders. The archive resembles the interior of a submarine, an unimaginably huge library aboard Captain Nemo's wonderful *Nautilus*. The air is chilly, the fans are humming, and the humidifiers are percolating discreetly.

Kim is searching for something, walking down the corridors for late nineteeth- and turn-of-the-century pictures. She slows at August 9, 1902, "The Coronation of King Edward VII and Queen Alexandra" and August 1905, "The Arrest of Christabel Pankhurst and Annie Kenney". After "Mass Meeting with Leading Socialist Keir Hardie before Reforming the Labour Party", she stops, checking the folders for 1905, then 1906. She lightly climbs one of the ladders and brings down two worn black archive boxes.

"These were in the police collections at Old Scotland Yard, part of a case from 1906," she explains. "Most of the evidence was photographic. We keep not only the pictures but also a summary of the investigation, explaining its history and the provenance of the images. I've been through the whole case once, but had forgotten about it until now. Actually, this is Neil's area of special interest."

She puts the boxes on a metal table and opens them. The first one contains photos of different sizes, single or bound into booklets. Some are as small as the cigarette cards that became popular at the time, nice little collectable items. All are of children.

"It wasn't just Charles Dodgson who liked taking pictures of naked kids," she says, slowly arranging the photos in row after row on the tabletop. "Compared with what people traffic in nowadays, these look pretty innocent, but the background trade was just as fucking awful as it is now. Or worse. These cards were picked up during a raid on a bookstall in Charing Cross Station, where they were kept in a storage space round the back. A little something for 'Travelling Gentlemen with Special Interests'. There were whole albums given over to 'named' boys and girls, called things like Puck, Rosalie, Romeo, Miranda. If a customer took a particular fancy to someone, discreet meetings could be arranged. The children came from the big slums, often from crowded orphanages, and were good for only one thing – at least in the opinion of the gentlemen. No more than goods in a lucrative marketplace.

"When the police finally decided to act, the children were gone. Many had probably died. It had taken almost a year to make the decision to carry out the raids, it seems. The shopkeeper ended up in prison, of course, and may have been executed, I don't know. Anyway, nothing happened to the customers. Some were highly placed gentlemen. Rumour had it that at least one Cabinet Minister had been involved. This was a big scandal, just in time for the Christmas pantomime season too."

I pick up some of the cards, examining them one by one.

The children were thin-faced, their bodies undernourished. It's hard to see what the attraction was. Not that it's much use trying to understand something so incomprehensible.

A pale little Miranda. No loving father though.

Among the few lines from Shakespeare that I remember are these, spoken by Miranda in *The Tempest*: "O, wonder! How many goodly creatures are there here! How beauteous mankind is! O brave new world, That has such people in't!" Jacob used to read aloud to me from the plays in an old translation, bound in worn leather that smelled sweetly of decay. I liked *The Tempest*, the story of shipwrecked people who return home. It's a fairy tale about nature confronting culture. During Shakespeare's life, it was performed at the Blackfriars Theatre in front of raucous, violent audiences who would just as soon have watched a bloody dogfight or an execution. Jacob said he'd seen it once in London, "a very long time ago". He loved reading the plays with lots of feeling.

I wonder how much he remembered about this kind of thing. Could anyone ever forget it?

*

Kim picks up another mounted photocard and examines it carefully. The print on the back simply reads *Quality Productions*.

"Cards like this were on sale in lots of places – Soho streets and shady lanes behind the big West End theatres. Nice contrast – there was Ellen Terry on stage inside, holding forth about the noblest sentiments, but in the shadows outside this trafficking was going on. It was part of the city's 'entertainment' scene, but hidden away. Then, as now, there was lots of money in child prostitution."

Kim collects the photos to put them back in their dark box.

"Then what happened?" I ask. "Apart from that Charing Cross shop-keeper, did they get hold of any of the other guilty parties?"

"Nobody much, as far as I know. Some street vendors. Oh, and a handful of children, who were either sent to orphanages or shut away in poorhouses, if thought to be too depraved. A lucky few were looked after by philanthropic societies and apparently adopted in the end.

"Anyway, the customers used fake names too, like Macbeth or the Count of Ortranto, and no-one was ever caught in the act. There was no evidence that would stand up in court. The complicated network that handled production and distribution was never unpicked. It's doubtful if anyone really tried. The key people must have acted through chains of middlemen, mainly from the working class – people with debts or maybe just easy-going consciences.

"The most powerful customers naturally looked after each other. It was unlikely that any of them would have been conscience-stricken enough to come forward and confess. The Edwardians, at least among the upper classes, found the exploitation of children in factories, in appalling conditions, perfectly acceptable, but were outraged by the sexual exploitation of children in the streets. Someone finally leaked the truth, and everything stopped for a while. The informant was anonymous, even in the police reports."

Suddenly and soundlessly, Neil McGowan materialises from behind us. Even Kim is startled, though she should be used to him by now. Neil looks critically at us, fumbling in his pocket to produce a sheet of paper.

"I've been in touch with Weymouth, and they've faxed us quite a lot of info about the Frobishers, Alice and Max," he says. "Alice is still well known locally, quite famous as a landscape artist. They call her stuff 'light painting in an expressive spirit'. Her oils and watercolours fetch very good prices. There's a gallery in Southampton that has a lot of her work, but some of her most highly regarded paintings are privately owned. For instance, *Woman by the Sea* is with a Brighton collector. Alice died in 1955, having survived her husband for a long time. Max was a GP and died in 1929. In 1907, they adopted a girl called Dora Flaherty. No notes about her until she caught measles in 1909. Weymouth actually checked Frobisher's case-notes, but the folders for 1907 and 1908 have disappeared."

Neil, obviously disapproving, sucks his teeth and starts reading again.

"Dora Frobisher, as she was then, died in 1918. The cause was Spanish influenza, and there are some more comments on the death certificate. Not by Frobisher, but by some other doctor. Here's a copy."

He hands me the fax. Someone had filled in the 1918 death certificate with quick, rather careless handwriting. The ink was smudged in several places.

"Discolouration of skin", I manage to read. "Cyanosis. Inflamed heart muscle". The rest is medical Latin and impossible to decipher.

Neil is ready with an explanation.

"Cyanosis was also called 'blue sickness'. The inflammation meant that the heart muscle wasn't getting enough oxygen and . . . the sufferer suffocated, in effect."

"Is this all they had?" I ask.

Neil shrugs.

"So it seems. You could always go to Brighton and take a look at Alice's home. She lived there in later years."

August 9 and 10, 1905

J ACOB FIRST MET Albert outside the stage entrance to the Drury Lane Theatre. Albert, working there as a stagehand, had seen Jacob waiting in the lane on many a night, hoping to catch a glimpse of Ellen Terry or one of the other actors and actresses. The theatre should have been closed for the summer, but the King was in London, and performances had been laid on for the Court and his many friends.

Rumours were going around to the effect that the Kaiser was in town on a secret visit to have a chat with his uncle about the situation in Russia. Kaiser Wilhelm loved the theatre as much as parades.

After seeing Jacob several times, Albert decided to approach him. Offering his new friend a mean-looking, unevenly rolled cigarette made with tobacco from Virginia, he informed him that he'd seen "dear old Mrs Craig – yeah, that's what Miss Terry is called off-stage – and Mr Henry Irving, while he was still alive". Albert's own favourite star was Mary Lloyd, who was on at the Hippodrome, where he had seen her on many occasions. He whistled the refrain of "My Old Man Said Follow the Van" and took a few swaying dance steps in the dark alley. "Mind you, if I'd done that in the theatre it would've meant bad luck," he said.

Albert, named after Queen Victoria's eldest son and just past his 19th birthday, still looked boyish despite the narrow moustache he was cultivating. From time to time, he stroked it as if to reassure himself that it was still there. His mane of brown hair grew in soft curls, and his eyelashes were as long and thick as a girl's.

This warm summer's night, they struck up an easy conversation, talking for a long time as if they already knew each other well.

Albert told Jacob that his great ambition was to join the Royal Guards. Maybe he'd have a chance if the war would only come quickly. He invited Jacob back-stage. Jacob's first impression was of a hot and dusty place filled with girls, all of whom giggled as they squeezed past him. The odour of powder, sweat and dry old wood filled his nostrils.

Albert showed him how the heavy curtain was raised and dropped on thick ropes running over huge greased pulleys "like the tight rigging on a man-o'-war". The counterweights, designed to keep the complex system of flats in place, were jute sacks filled with sand. Depending on how they were painted, the flats could be used to turn the stage into any place at all, he explained – Prince Hamlet's dark castle or the stormy grey waves in *The Tempest*.

"Old seadogs were great for working stage machinery – they were used to handling ropes, and besides, they didn't seem to mind staying crouched in the stale air beneath the boards. But theatre managers realised that the sailors got pissed all the time and didn't take the staging seriously. They just hauled out whatever was at hand, using the dark Scottish moors intended for *Macbeth* as a backdrop for a comedy by Gilbert and Sullivan."

Albert nods, reflecting on the depth of his own knowledge, but he loses some of his composure when he is shown Jacob's camera. It's a modern Press camera with automatic shutter. He points the lens playfully at Jacob, and inside the camera the shutter opens and reveals its empty room.

*

It was already past midnight when Jacob walked down Drury Lane towards the Strand. He had to spend the night in Burrows's studio, because his landlady would have locked up and gone to bed long since. He hoped Burrows would still be there and sober enough to let him in.

His way took him past Trafalgar Square, where new posters had been put up around the bases of the lion statues urging the public to protest against the arrests of the Suffragettes Christabel Pankhurst and Annie Kenney. Jacob had met Mrs Pankhurst once at Annie Besant's house and could not imagine her or her two daughters in Holloway Prison. She had looked so fragile, almost birdlike. Stopping to read the posters, he noted that the Suffragettes were calling for a demonstration outside Buckingham Palace.

Then he looked up. There were lines of trees planted along the pavements, straight rows of saplings looking more like fence-posts than growing plants. The narrow trunks had a silvery sheen in the darkness. Suddenly, the great forests of his native land came to mind. He remembered the air, clear and fresh and somehow unfathomable like a deep forest tarn. He remembered a warped rainwater barrel next to his family's summerhouse on an island not far from Gothenburg harbour. The water's smell was always pure, but it had a metallic edge reminding him of phosphorus and sea-salt. If you washed in it, the slight scent of burning stayed on your skin.

The two fountains in Trafalgar Square spouted city water, cloudy and dull with bubbles of tough, greyish foam rising to the surface.

*

Frightened by Jacob's footfalls, a few filthy pigeons flapped away, disturbing a ragged man sleeping rough in the square. The bells of St Martin-in-the-Fields chimed the half-hour. Jacob thought of how close he was to the heart of the British Empire and of how, all around him, an unceasing tide of mumbling sounds flowed from the city that never slept.

Carriages were backing up along Fleet Street, which echoed with the rattling of wheels and the neighing of fed-up, exhausted horses, interrupted now and then by the staccato sounds of automobile engines. Heavily made-up prostitutes with shrill voices were emerging from their dank Soho attics to earn a crust by working the streets for yet another night. Wafts of cigar smoke and perfume mingled with the familiar smell of horse manure.

Jacob was aware that near him, close enough to be touched, the forgotten hordes of the unemployed, the old and the sick were on the move, forced to drag themselves through the streets until morning, when they could look for somewhere to sleep in the parks. He had seen these things more clearly since he'd read Jack London's reports in the papers. Not that everyone liked these stories. There had been plenty of Letters to the Editor complaining about that Yankee and his wretched bellyaching.

A scene from earlier that night came to mind. Two gentlemen in top hats and tails, presumably just out from the theatre, had been chatting up two sailors. Then all four men walked calmly off together, the gentlemen's shirtfronts and the sailors' blouses shining white under the streetlamps.

*

Albert and Jacob had ended up talking outside a pub called The Seven Bells. A shabbily dressed man had tried to sell them something looking like packets of photographs, but Albert had addressed him by name, told him off and shooed him away.

In spite of the pub door being open to the summer night, the air in The Seven Bells was hot and foul with tobacco smoke, body odours and the penetrating tang of sour spilt beer and vomit. Somebody had thrown up just inside the door, and Jacob had slipped in the mess, much to Albert's amusement.

Trying to rub off the worst of it with his handkerchief and water from the privy tap was not a success. The handkerchief was ruined, of course, and Jacob's shoes and trouser leg still smelled. The pub privy was a cramped space with a tap and a stinking piss-gutter, but clearly not nasty enough to put off a bear-like man who tried to push Jacob against the wall. The man's breath was a powerful mix of gin and raw spirits. Jacob managed to escape, mainly because the man collapsed in a drunken stupor. Jacob fled, grateful that he had left his camera with Albert.

*

It was too late for the newsboy minding the *Daily Mail* stall at Charing Cross Station; he had fallen asleep next to the poster announcing yesterday's news: "PEACE TREATY SIGNED NEXT MONTH! RUSSIA DEFEATED. JAPAN – NEW GREAT POWER IN THE EAST." The front of the station was quiet and empty apart from the waiting carriages. Both coachmen and horses were sleeping on the hoof. Even the beggars had gone to hole up for the night.

On an impulse, Jacob wandered into the station. With his clothes in the state they were he felt ashamed even to face Burrows at the studio. The air in the great concourse was hotter than in the street and vibrating with steam from the enormous black locomotives standing still but breathing heavily like stranded whales. The platform vaults resounded to the dull notes struck by a man checking their huge wheels, paired by the brakes that held them still. He hit each one with a hammer in order to pick up any cracked notes, any hints of metal fatigue hidden inside the gleaming wheel perimeters and smoothly oiled gears. He rubbed his sweaty face from time to time, using a filthy rag that merely left a paler trace on his blackened face. He looked like an Indian brave in war paint, but also like a monkey, agile and aware as he clambered over buffers and hoses.

*

Jacob looked up. The vaults were so complex, a web of steel arches and glass obscured by the dense, grey air. The platforms stretched ahead like quays, opening up vistas into the unknown. In the distance rose rough, smoke-stained brick walls over the tracery of steel tracks glistening against the oily blackness of the embankments. He was tempted by the idea of travel. He imagined being pulled away by one of these black monsters breathing out clouds of steam, leaving everything behind him to go to Vienna or Berlin or . . . Then he reminded himself that he already was far from home.

He had a vision of his brother Felix, who had thrown up every time he had to travel. Felix, his skin pale and almost yellow, would sneak in and out of the toilet while trying to pretend that nothing was wrong. Later in life, he would fuss like an old woman about his luggage and harass the servants every time he had to travel to Copenhagen or

Kristiania by train in aid of their father's business. His anxiety peaked when he had to take a ship to Hull across the rough waters of the North Sea. On his return, he would always claim to be starving and insist on having creamy dishes and the richest cuts of pork for supper.

Oddly, although Felix always ate a lot and quickly, scraping his plate, he was always thinner than Jacob.

*

The ticket office hatches were closed and barred. A solitary traveller was sleeping, leaning against his trunk. The huge clock face above the concourse showed 12.50 a.m. The lavatories were closed against night-time vandals, even though a police constable built like a prize-fighter was doing the rounds. He gazed inquisitively at Jacob for a moment and then marched heavily off to patrol the platforms.

Security was high because the Suffragettes had become more militant, and the most desperate cadres seemed capable of any outrage against public property. The Irish were becoming more difficult as well. Their demand for Home Rule had caused Prime Minister Balfour a great deal of trouble in Parliament. And then there were the anarchists. Only the previous week, the police had managed to break up one of their cells. The plotters had been based in an East End tenement flat by Commercial Road, complete with a sizeable hoard of dynamite. Maybe the long, hot summer had something to do with all of this disquiet, glowing and occasionally flaring up like a flame long hidden under an old roof.

*

A shop next to the ticket office was still open. The slate board with advertisements written on it in chalk presented an assortment of tobacco goods, cheap tin toys, groceries, popular books like Elinor Glyn's daring novels, brushes with real bristles and toiletries. Next to the board was a gaslight with a red glass cover rather clumsily shaped to look like a hand holding a torch. Its light gave the shop display an unreal air, like limelight on a garish stage set.

A man appeared at Jacob's elbow. His head was round and absolutely bald, and he wore an eyeshade resembling the traditional headgear of printers.

"Interesting, isn't it, Sir? That's a copy of the hand of the Statue of Liberty, a most imposing work of art in New York City, as I'm sure you're aware."

In spite of the warm weather, the man was wearing a black waist-coat and jacket, carefully buttoned over his fat belly, and drops of sweat lodged among the black stubble on his cheeks. The air in the narrow shop felt unbearably hot and still. The walls were stacked high with cardboard boxes, and Jacob's eye was caught by one containing Pear's soap with its trademark colour picture of an angelic little boy with forget-me-not blue eyes.

"I'd like a bar of soap, one of those. Can you let me use a wash-basin? I'd pay, of course."

He felt sticky and dirty. The smell of vomit was becoming notice-able in the hot shop. The man looked right at him, appraising him carefully.

"Very well, Sir. But if I've got to clean up after you, it'll cost you a pound."

His voice was educated and unaccented, but he seemed to speak with an effort, enunciating with the exaggerated care of someone who had learned to speak English as an adult. Jacob remembered his brother's contempt for "money-grubbing Jews" and told himself that the chap might well be Russian or from one of these little warring states in the Balkans. Fleetingly, he wondered if he too sounded alien, but comforted himself with the thought that his father had insisted on speaking English at home.

But a pound was half his weekly rent. He had already spent too much that month, what with going to the theatre and paying for rounds in the pub. He had bought books, sketchpads and decent pencils. His father would disapprove of any begging letters. The little boy on the soapbox eyed him indifferently, and the shopkeeper, noticing his hesitation, softened a bit.

"Come on, young Sir, half that for the tidy use of soap and water – that's not unreasonable."

His voice sounded ironic. Jacob looked down, embarrassed, and realised that his shoes were covered in something disgusting, a dark, slimy substance. Was it blood? Maybe the man in the pub privy had been injured. He had collapsed and stayed down, immobile. Jacob had left as fast as he could, paying no attention to the man's condition.

If it was blood, that decided matters. He handed the shopkeeper some money and followed him into the back of the shop.

*

The washroom's tiny, filthy window had been propped open on a rusty hook. Jacob climbed up on a stool that had been used for the same purpose before, judging by the dirty footprints on it, and peered outside. The window looked out over a hidden, deserted part of the station whose only feature was a group of disused railway carriages. In the dark distance gaped the deeper black interior of a tunnel, the opening marked by a single lamp. Not a soul was moving out there.

He looked around the washroom, which was tidy and clean but very basic. Apart from the stool, there was a wooden bench, a tin basin and bucket, a china jug full of water and a shelf. On the shelf was a tin of rat poison.

The "Russian" appeared with a large kettle of hot water. Jacob was appalled to see the water turn red when he dipped his hands in the basin. Although his light linen jacket was unstained, there was blood on both his waistcoat and his trousers. The man in the pub must have been bleeding from his stomach. Why hadn't he and Albert noticed? Instead, they had finished their pints and left the place.

Jacob washed and washed, changing the water over and over again, revolted by the smell of vomit and with the metallic odour of blood. In the end, he scrubbed his hands until the skin was smarting and red. At least they smelled sweetly of lavender now. There was no drain, so he decided to empty the dirty water in the yard. There was still no-one in sight – no-one, that is, except the house martins, diving and swooping with fluid elegance in the warm night. They must have had their nests high up on the wall where bricks had fallen out. The sight moved Jacob almost to tears. It seemed so peaceful, so full of innocent grace.

He tried to think, but his thoughts moved slowly, fishing for decisions in the turgid stream of his consciousness. He must find Albert and ask if he had noticed or heard anything that night.

That's what he must do. If only he weren't feeling so utterly exhausted. His mind would not settle down. The same questions kept coming back to him. Was the man dead? Just injured? But abdominal wounds were dangerous, he knew that. Round and round went his thoughts. If he went back to check if the man was still there, would he be suspected of foul play? Had anybody seen him?

He tried to go back over his movements that night. If only he could see it all again, observe all the details. His memory remained blurred. The room had been filled with people in various states of intoxication, drinking, smoking and arguing. Some had been gambling – throwing dice, playing card-games or dominoes. He could remember hearing the counters clicking on a nearby table. There had been a mirror in an ornate frame, but Jacob had never looked at himself. He usually feared that all of his carefully built up confidence would be lost if he caught sight of himself looking too childish and inexperienced. In fact, no-one had paid any attention to him. No-one, that is, except a middle-aged lady who had patted his cheek. But then, her eyes had been bleary with drink, and she was surely not going to remember him.

Albert, now, he was important. Jacob hardly knew him, but even so he would surely have said something about the blood. He must have seen it. But he had only handed Jacob a handkerchief and gestured towards the door to signify that it was time to go.

*

The piercing sound of a train's whistle ripped through the tangled threads of Jacob's thoughts. The night train from the north was coming

in, trailing clouds of steam. Jacob checked his watch and was horri-
fied to see that it was 2.30 a.m. He pulled on his damp clothes, feeling
grateful for the warm weather. He had to sleep for a few hours. Stop
thinking.

Going through to the front of the shop, he noticed a space that
resembled Burrow's darkroom. It had black blinds, stacks of metal
dishes and rows of dark-painted bottles. He wondered whether the
businesslike "Russian" went in for photography too. Standing in the
concourse looking for customers, the shopkeeper barely noticed Jacob
as he passed.

*

By 3 a.m., Jacob was back at The Seven Bells. Dawn was breaking over
the grey, dusty city. The pub was shut and silent, the street deserted.
Burrows called the small hours of the morning "the city's time of rest".

The old landscape would rise up again each morning, like a ghostly
reminder of the past. An ancient map would be redrawn as the cool,
pale mist floated once more over the old wetlands of the Thames
Valley. It was at its densest in the vanished ravines where streams had
once danced along twisting, pebble-strewn beds, and around the lower
reaches of the hills, where the early valley people had buried chief-
tains and their women under cairns of carefully selected stones.

These, long since paved over, lay deep in the city's dead soil. As
the mist crawled along the dark, quiet street, Jacob felt chilled in his
damp clothes. In the lane behind The Seven Bells, he dragged a dustbin
up against the wall. Standing on it, he was able to see the pub's yard.
It was full of barrels, broken boxes and every kind of rubbish. No
windows seemed to overlook the yard, only blank firewalls. A limping
mongrel saw him and whined and wagged its tail. Jacob jumped down
into the yard, carefully avoiding the broken bricks.

The dog was delighted, barking and licking his trouser legs enthusiastically. It was quite large, part-Alsatian with beautiful pointy ears
that had been badly scratched and torn in fights with feral cats.
Heyman the cobbler, who lived in their courtyard house in Gothenburg,

kept a better-cared-for version of a German shepherd. This dog was just as affectionate, and when Jacob whispered to it to be quiet, it seemed to understand straight away. Maybe it was silly, but the dog made him feel less lonely. The rough chain round its neck trailed the torn end of a rope, so someone must have kept the animal on a leash.

Jacob stood up and looked round the yard. There was a broken-down cart, a trough and several empty barrows probably waiting to be taken back to the brewery. Clouds of fat bluebottles were feasting on sour pools of spilt beer, live insects clambering greedily over drowned ones. Their low humming almost lulled him to sleep.

He cautiously made his way towards the pub's back door, followed by the dog. Though it was growling with its ears laid back, it didn't seem to mind Jacob. The privy door was badly warped and closed only by a padlock on a long chain. Was this terrifying guard-dog meant to frighten intruders away?

Jacob leaned forward to peer through the gap between the frame and the door. The privy was empty. The ammonia smell of urine stung his nose. The dog had backed away, its fur standing on end. When Jacob's eyes became accustomed to the dark, he noticed that the privy floor was gleaming as if it had been washed recently and with some care. There was no trace of the bleeding man, and if it hadn't been for the dog's obvious fear, Jacob might have given up looking.

By now, the dog had run off to stand by the gate to the yard, rubbing one of its front legs against the wood. Jacob felt in his pockets for the thin-bladed knife he used to cut open the thick greaseproof envelopes that protected photographic plates. Checking nervously that his camera hung securely round his neck, he began probing with the tip of the knife inside the padlock. It turned out to be easy to find the hook holding the crossbar in place, but the mechanism was stiff with rust and lack of use.

Once inside, he was almost knocked backwards by the stench. There was no trace of blood on the floor or in the air. He tried but failed to recall what the injured man had looked like. The darkness and confusion had only left the memory of alcohol-stinking breath mixed with the quieter note of something fresh and rural, an impression of a life spent outdoors.

A fat spider had spun its web across the small window. It hung there, a small, fleshy being, contemplating a few drops of water caught in the threads. Jacob realised that the walls must have been washed down as well. By now, the dog had crept closer, its tail tucked between its legs. It stared at Jacob, its large eyes glowing yellow. He tried to talk to it gently, but the animal wouldn't be calmed. It stayed where it was, sniffing at the edge of the wet floor. The light had become strong enough for Jacob to see that one of its front legs had been cut.

"You don't belong round here, do you?" he asked it quietly. The dog shook itself, whining a little.

Jacob pushed the bar-room door open with infinite caution. Nobody had made the slightest effort to tidy up there. No-one had wiped up the spilt brandy or righted the fallen chairs and tables or found a brush and pan to sweep up the glittering shards of broken glass. The silence was broken by the shockingly loud drip from a tap into a tin bucket. Jacob stepped carefully to avoid the worst spills. He did not want to leave any footprints. There was not a soul about, but the windows to the street were large, and there were distant noises of the neighbourhood coming to life. Gruff voices, sober and therefore grim, called out sleepily, answering a woman's taunting laughter with bad-tempered swearing. The morning had grown very bright.

The dog was waiting for him. He bent over it, stroking its powerful head. Then he realised that what he had thought was dirt was actually blood dried into its fur. He took a closer look at the injury, a shallow cut that needed cleaning soon. He decided to take the dog with him.

He had to find something to stand on to climb out of the yard again. The barrels seemed the best bet. The nearest lot were of intense interest to a cloud of particularly fat, shimmering bluebottles. The noise they made sounded like reverberations in a closed space, echoing and monotonous. Sensing damp on his face, the swarm moved in on Jacob, and he flailed about to get rid of them. Picking the sturdiest-looking barrel, he lifted the stout lid and grabbed the barrel's edge to turn it over.

*

The dead man had been forced into the barrel by folding him into a foetal position. The smell of wilderness still hung around the dead man, as it did around what must be his dog, but it was overwhelmed by a stomach-turning mix of fermenting beer, vomit and dried blood. The man's hair was long and a rich, deep blond that still looked implausibly alive against his waxen skin. Someone had brought his fingers together on the torn, patched knees of his trousers, as if in prayer. The clasped hands and the man's utter stillness made Jacob feel respectful.

Looking at the body more closely, he saw the bluing bruises and broken skin over the dead man's knuckles and cheekbones. One hand was still gripping the end of a torn rope, the skin discoloured at the edges. This had to be the other end of the dog's lead.

The practically solid cloud of flies never left them alone. Jacob saw that some were already crawling in and out between the corpse's pale lips and half-closed eyelids. He turned away to vomit until nothing but bile was left inside him. The dog seemed sympathetic, buffing him now and then with its moist, eager nose.

There was a pump in the yard, and he let the cool water flow over his head and hands. Then he made his hands into a bowl for the dog to drink from. It greedily licked up every drop. Meanwhile, he tried to think. The dog must have got away, hiding in the dark. The people who had tidied up the privy were likely to come back for it. He must hurry.

Reluctantly, he returned to the corpse. There was something hanging round the man's neck on a worn leather strap. With shaking hands, Jacob cut the strap with his knife, pulling the object clear of the body, which was as stiff and hard as a piece of wood. The hungry, irritated flies seemed determined to do everything to stop him. The object turned out to be a tatty leather wallet roughly branded with the initials M. F.

Jacob took a last look at the man's face. He felt sure that he had seen him before, and recently. To be precise, the previous night at the house in Lansdowne Road.

*

They had been holding one of the sessions Mrs Besant liked to call "spiritual meetings". "Frankly," she would say, "one can't use the word 'seance' any more; it reeks of sensationalism and silly party games." Jacob had turned up at 6 p.m.; they were due to start at 7.00 because old Miss Clark didn't like being out after nightfall. Jacob's job was to set up the camera in good time and see that the photographer had everything he needed. Annie Besant herself had opened the door. The pale little girl was nowhere to be seen.

Mme Blavatsky's unwieldy Russian samovar had been placed in the middle of the table, polished to a high sheen, filled and ready to be lit. Mrs Besant had put burning sticks of Indian incense round the drawing room, and the heavy curtains had been drawn. The scent of the joss sticks was heavy, a mixture of sandalwood, patchouli, saffron and myrrh. Later, Jacob would light the candles.

While he rigged up the tripod and got the rest of the equipment in order, Mrs Besant told him about her stay in India, an unimaginably enormous, unbelievably hot and unbearably dusty place. When trains crossed the huge plains, the powdery red soil crept into the stale air of the compartments, filling every crevice – one's eyes, nose and mouth – until one thought one was suffocating. The food tasted of the red earth too. She spoke of droughts followed by terrible rains that went on forever and drowned everything.

There were thousands upon thousands of homeless Indian children who lived in the streets of terrible, smelly, hellishly noisy cities. No-one cared for them; they were dirty, miserable, crawling with vermin and prey to repulsive diseases. Begging in the streets like dogs was their only means of survival. Yes, indeed – the poverty was much worse than anything Jacob would have seen in London, worse than anything he could ever imagine.

She had experienced so much. She had visited Kaligat, near

Calcutta, and sacrificed a kid to the goddess Kali, also called "The Black One". Well, the kid had been dead already. She had studied the exceedingly erotic – very, very improper – wall paintings in the temple of Shiva at the sacred site of Benares and attended the burning of corpses on the muddy shores of the equally sacred Ganges. Sometimes when the fires went out too soon, half-burnt bodies floated downriver and washed up along the shore. Dogs usually found these remains, mauled them badly and, if they were starving, fed on the flesh – at least, the story was that it was dogs that did this.

Yes, India was unforgettable; the memories were deeply etched in her mind and were always brought back by the smell of incense.

*

A little later, Mrs Besant withdrew to "collect her thoughts". By 6.30, there was a knock on the door, and Jacob went to open it. The man whose body he later found in the barrel was standing outside, looking determined and earnest, almost solemn. He was wearing a jacket of coarse wool, and his hair was tucked under a round knitted hat of the kind sailors wore. Here and there, strong, blond strands stuck out. His broad face looked open and pleasant, the skin dark from weather and wind. He was alone, so he must have left the dog somewhere.

The man asked for Dora and Tom, saying that they were his children. He had been given to understand that they lived here. Jacob called Mrs Besant, who led the man to her study, closing the door behind them. He had seemed perfectly sober but elated, even happy. His accent made it obvious that, like Annie Besant, he came from Ireland. He must have left without Jacob noticing. Mrs Besant seemed paler than usual, and disturbed.

The session that evening was unsatisfactory – or at least took a most unusual turn.

*

There had been five people round the table, five pairs of hands reaching out under the black silk tablecloth and gripping their neighbours' hands as if their owners were drowning.

These people were old-timers with a set routine that helped them to feel strong and concentrate. First, they drank many cups of strong Russian tea and ate large quantities of small, hard biscuits, made very spicy with ginger, cumin, anise and one other, secret ingredient which gave them a bitter, slightly harsh but fresh aftertaste, almost like eating uncooked rhubarb or gooseberries. This was one of Madame's secret recipes, a powerful concoction that made elderly hearts beat steadily and minds sharpen up.

*

Almost 70 years old, Miss Phyllida Clark was the oldest member of the group. Her fiancé had disappeared from her life almost fifty years earlier. Having been involved in India's Sepoy Rebellion in 1857, he was thought to have fallen at Lucknow. As it happened, Miss Clark's family had strong connections with India and had been running an import-export business which involved monopolies on some very profitable goods. In the fullness of time, Miss Clark had inherited a respectable fortune. She always took a lively interest in Mrs Besant's stories from "that wild, awful place", as she put it.

Next to Phyllida Clark sat Colonel Jack Rider, once very much a man of action, uncompromising and hard – or that had seemed a fair assessment until his son George had been shot at Bloemfontein in 1901. Although reluctant to begin with, he was now quite willing to spend an evening holding hands with people like Phyllida Clark in the name of human kindness. When war with Russia had seemed inescapable after the unfortunate Dogger Bank episode, Colonel Rider had sent several strong letters to his MP, arguing crisply in favour of peace.

Next to the Colonel sat Miss Heather Brown, a striking woman in her 40s. She had written several successful books under a male pseudonym. Her visits to the Besant circle were driven by a need to come to terms with a secret sorrow. Heather Brown was in mourning for her lifelong love, but could not grieve openly because her dead partner was a woman. Since no-one in society would be scandalised by her interest in spirits, she felt that these sessions gave justified relief for someone turned mute by convention. She was a born sceptic and had joined the seances with an attitude of amused reservation. Still, Heather Brown and Annie Besant went a long way back. They had got to know and like each other in the women's rights movement, particularly during the long campaign for the right to control fertility.

The fourth member of the group that night was none other than W. T. Stead, a devotee with a genuine interest in the occult. He also liked attractive women and was squeezing Heather's and Annie's slender hands with equal enthusiasm. That night, Jacob was thrilled by Stead's gift of a roll of film.

These people belonged to Annie's "core group" which was sometimes joined by new arrivals wanting to solve emotional problems or simply satisfy their curiosity.

*

The group had been chatting about the weather. Annie Besant said that the heat was as bad as anything she'd experienced in India. Why, it reminded her of nights spent in the mission house at Adyar, when everyone stayed out on the veranda playing bridge or whist since sleep was impossible until the cool time just before dawn. The summer heat had returned to London after a short but violent storm. When the rain stopped, the ground had simply soaked up the water, releasing some in the form of a white mist, making visibility almost as poor as in the smoke-laden fogs of winter.

Annie always liked to begin with relaxing small talk accompanying the strong tea and cakes. Everywhere in the room candles were burning, their flames still even though the French windows to the garden were wide open. Phyllida Clark, feeling very sticky and hot, found herself staring straight into the slanted, taunting eyes of the Shiva figurine on the brass smoking table. The god was dancing, his eight arms reaching out in all directions and making Phyllida think of a nest of snakes or, better, an octopus. He seemed to want to *grasp everybody, to hold them tight*. The small figure was made of some black tropical wood carved to a smoothness resembling polished stone. Annie had said that the wood was so hard and dense that it couldn't catch fire, but at times Phyllida felt certain there was a tiny blue flame burning from each of the eight sets of fingers.

Jack Rider too was suffering from the airless heat, feeling just as uncomfortable as the old dear next to him. He regretted having come. The damned thing was, he needed to tell George that he loved him. He'd been a bloody insensitive father, frightened to speak of emotion in case it made the lad even more of a mummy's boy. Every time he came here, he thought the sound of sobbing hung in the air, as if someone was doomed to sadness.

Heather Brown was watching Annie, who was still fully conscious. Then her old friend's face began to change, and her beloved's face emerged in its place. Elisabeth had had strong features with a long, straight nose and high cheekbones. Heather had loved to follow the contours of those bones, her fingers moving with calming gentleness. She kept blinking, but her vision of the dead woman remained. Elisabeth's skin had yellowed towards the end, her eyes surrounded by dark shadows, and Heather was certain that this apparition had the same skin. When *the image of Elisabeth* turned towards her, she could not bear to look at it any more. When she dared to open her eyes again, it was gone.

William Stead, on the other hand, had been looking into the distance all the time, as if his thoughts were far away. Under his pleasant manner lurked some unexpressed worry.

*

Annie kept talking about India, but more and more slowly, her voice becoming deeper as if it was coming from somewhere else. Jacob moved closer to listen. She spoke of storytellers and astrologers, of those who could dream the truth or interpret dreams – holy men who starved themselves for weeks, chewing betel and aromatic leaves. They could transform themselves into animals, maybe birds or wild dogs, using these shapes to travel to the world of the spirits to ask the dead for advice. This practice drew on ancient beliefs still held in the villages of India, remnants of a religion that had existed long before the worship of Shiva and Kali. The gurus walked the countryside, but were often accused of heresy and driven away by local priests. Still, it did happen that people dreamed of animals, maybe birds or dogs, in the night after one of these men – call them what you would, dream travellers or magicians – had turned up at the village meeting-place. Then no-one could doubt that the dead were trying to tell the dreamers something.

*

Annie's voice got fainter. A clock struck 8.00 somewhere in the house. Phyllida cleared her throat nervously.

What happened next was unearthly, elusive. No-one was able to describe it properly afterwards.

A small boy appeared in the centre of the room. He was very pale. His body, clothed in a torn shirt and a pair of muddy, ill-fitting trousers, was distinctly outlined in the light. There was something else about him, a pulsating, crackling *presence* that ran through the silent room like an electrical current. His being seemed intensified by power drawn from the small, frightened group at the table. Even the candle flames seemed to shrink and fade, though they continued to burn calmly.

Behind the boy, the door stood open, as if he had entered and crossed the floor soundlessly and unnoticed. Loud noises and excited voices were heard elsewhere in the house, almost as if someone was crashing about and swearing. The next moment, Pastor Charles Leadbeater, in his shirtsleeves, came rushing into the room, and suddenly the pale little figure vanished, as mysteriously as it had appeared.

Then someone turned on the ceiling light, and they all blinked in confusion under the glare of the exposed bulbs. There was nothing to be seen, except possibly a stain made by dirty water on the floor and an odd smell of river mud and rotting vegetation.

*

Jack Rider stood up. He had been very upset by the apparition and didn't know what to think. His face was as white as the boy's had been, and his jaws were working without producing any words. The boy hadn't looked like George in the slightest and of course had been far too young anyway, but even so Rider felt an uncontrollable wave of loss and grief sweep through him. Leadbeater took no notice and turned to Annie, who was staring at him as confusedly as if she had just awakened from a deep, dreamless sleep.

"Annie, this is unbearable, I cannot work under these dreadful conditions. Kindly keep your philanthropic cases out of my way."

Leadbeater barely managed to control his voice, and his strong hands were still shaking. On their backs and on his thick, hairy fore-arms, the skin was flaky, red and slightly swollen, as if he had been working with them immersed in cold water. Leadbeater noticed this and swiftly clasped them behind him. The solemn philosophical stance and sonority of his voice were made a mockery by his sweat-stained shirt, rolled-up sleeves and stretched, yellowing braces.

Phyllida, who had recovered quite quickly, was observing him with the indiscreet curiosity that is the privilege of the old. He reminded her of her older brother Henry, who had died of typhoid in 1851. He had been a naughty boy – drowning cats in the millpond for fun – and was missed by no-one except their mother. His death had prevented Phyllida from going to the Great Exhibition held in Hyde Park that year.

Then the whole scene changed again. The blond man with the knitted cap appeared in the middle of the room and leapt at Leadbeater, growling – or so Heather Brown described it later.

It took the other men in the room a few moments to respond. The pastor was already blue in the face from lack of oxygen when Rider and Stead together managed to pull the assailant off him. The unknown man was almost supernaturally strong and moved round the room with the desperation and cunning of a cornered wild creature. He continued to abuse Leadbeater violently, seemingly utterly deranged. Rider and Stead were unable to force the madman to the floor or even hold him. He twisted free of their grip, vanishing into the garden with long, powerful strides. They tried to give chase, but found it impossible in the deep, dark shade. He was gone without a trace.

The rich vegetation gave off the warm, earthy scents of late summer. The surprisingly damp soil had been invaded everywhere by tree roots. William Stead had the fanciful impression that nature was moving in on the illuminated house.

*

"The man's insane; for God's sake let him be," Leadbeater wheezed. Annie and Heather had hauled him across the room to slump on a narrow settee, and colour was returning to his face. In fact, it looked almost as red as the port Annie was trying to make him drink. Even though she was attempting to help him, her movements were oddly stiff.

Jacob had been watching everything quietly, uncertain whether it was proper to become involved. He began to dismantle the camera equipment. At least he had five exposures, though the light had been very poor. He hadn't got round to using magnesium flares in the tumult. The pale boy had been running among the furniture looking for an escape, as small and swift as a grey rat. At one point, he had collided with Jacob's leg firmly enough to convince him that he was no ghost, whatever the others believed.

Stead told Jacob that he would take charge of the exposed film. He was an experienced newspaperman, after all, and considered himself competent enough to handle the developing. The results must not be put at risk by using the roll for more exposures, because it was well known that film could get stuck in a camera, jeopardising a whole session. Stead, still pale and sweating after his exertions, was very insistent and somehow nervous, Jacob thought. His eyes looked anxious, and silvery stubble covered his normally smoothly shaved cheeks.

*

Jacob held his breath when he thought he heard voices just outside the gate to the yard. Then it was silent again.

He had tied the cut strap of the dead man's wallet round his neck, and it hung there like a ghostly, cold weight, smelling badly even after a wash under the pump. Before investigating its contents, he had to get out of here, he thought. He started to rig up a platform of boxes and planks. No more barrels.

Then he gathered the dog up in his arms, and it clung to him, shivering and weakly wagging its tail, but staying quite still and making itself surprisingly light. Jacob heaved himself up on his elbows, aware of mortar cracking as he clambered over the top of the wall and on to the waiting dustbin on the other side.

The dog leapt to the ground and disappeared down the empty street, ignoring Jacob's calls.

Technicalities

I like experimenting with old photographic techniques. Photography has the power to preserve the present or, at least, to fix a particular moment in time. An agitated commentator once described the medium as humanity's attempt to "blasphemously conserve God's image".

*

In the 1840s and '50s, people started to experiment with solutions of silver salts (calotype), and, about a decade later, of platinum salts (platinotype). Egg-white, or albumen, was much used to bind salt solutions, and I have spent a lot of time trying to work with the albumen-silver technique favoured by people like Roger Fenton and Julia Margaret Cameron. (They modified a method devised by William Henry Fox Talbot in 1841.) The paper is prepared by soaking it first in a solution of common salt and then in a mixture of ammonia and silver nitrate. The negative is turned into a positive, direct-contact print by exposure to sunlight, often for hours on end. The contact between the positive and negative images means that a faint trace of the original paper's fibre-pattern stays within them.

The old daguerreotype positives existed only in single copies. Their precise detail has to be viewed through protective glass, because the images are sensitive to the slightest touch. Later technical innovations created more robust pictures that could be copied endlessly. Thus the mass production of images began. Initially, the albumen-silver process made for grainy, imprecise pictures, but quality improved by the end of the 1840s. The method was relatively simple. The egg-white and salt mixture was brushed onto high-quality paper made light-sensitive by an application of silver nitrate. For the first time, a mechanical, reproducible method to preserve "God's image" was created.

This method had a long lifespan. Albumen printing dominated the craft until the 1890s, when silver and gelatin printing took its place. The big disadvantage of the albumen method was that it devoured large quantities of egg whites to produce the paper. As many as six million eggs a year were used to make photographic images at the same time as one million people starved to death in Ireland during the Great Famine, and people were living in the great slums of Manchester, Liverpool and London – the very same people who built the wealth of the nation by working twelve hours a day on a diet of tea and bread. Paradoxically, it was the emergence of modern photography that brought the squalor into middle-class homes, thus bringing about social change.

*

Schllurrrrp – the water makes a hideous slurping noise as it drains from the basin through a narrow, rusty pipe.

I'm counting: one and two and . . . When I get to fifteen, I turn the canister once more, first sideways, cautiously, so that the developing fluid is distributed evenly over the rolled-up film with its tough, shiny coating.

I always develop my own negatives, wherever I am. I've repeated the familiar gestures and inhaled the pure, harsh scents of the chemicals in any number of small, windowless rooms. The excitement I feel is like waiting for a birth; there's the same sense of nervous anticipation.

20°C, 7½ minutes.

*

I've been working on the same project for many years now. I take pictures of houses, but not of entire buildings. It's the details I'm after. It could be a small cornerstone on which everything seems to rest, or some mark left by a tradesman, perhaps very long ago – cracks and scratches or even more personal signs like a brick that has retained the imprint of fingers from the moment when it was a piece of wet clay.

I pour out the developer and add fixative. The canister must be kept moving.

Room temperature for 10 minutes.

*

Below the flat I used to live in, a steep staircase went down to a cellar where I had set up a provisional darkroom. I worked for hours on getting my pictures right, but also tried to master old methods. I experimented with salt and silver, with surfaces that became smoothly reflective and resilient, capable of holding lots of details and transferring them to contact prints.

N* would sit waiting for me. When I came upstairs, she often declared war again, and the accusations would start flying. I was always the focus of old anger and concentrated bitterness. N* collected emotional states, keeping detailed documentation and hoarding the lot in thick albums of recorded family life.

We lived in Highgate Village. The house, built in 1870, had been James McNeil Whistler's refuge for a few months between travels. This alone increased the weekly rent by quite a bit. The rooms had plain white walls and were sparsely furnished. We had little to add by way of personal possessions. The owner had hung a Hokusai reproduction on the wall over our hard bed. It was called *The Hollow of the Deep Sea Wave off Kanagawa*. He had been visiting Japan for many years and had exquisite, minimalist taste.

N* and I tended to take turns going out. I would take a camera, preferably the Hasselblad, and amble along the narrow, winding village streets that run steeply down the hill and once caused horse-drawn carriages such problems. Highgate was isolated on top of its hill back in those days, the great city distant and half-hidden in a bluish haze against which spires and towers were reduced to black lines. The old

Highgate Cemetery, a stretch of woodland with scattered graves, was a favourite haunt of mine. Roaming about in the dense green shade was like finding your way through an unfathomable, leafy labyrinth.

There were gravestones I went to see again and again. One had been raised in memory of a 12-year-old boy who had fallen to his death in northern Sweden on July 2, 1902. He had been diving from "Finn Rock in Dalarna Province". They must have brought his body back by steamship in the heat of high summer.

*

I start siphoning the fixative into a container on the floor, following it with clear water at room temperature. The rinsing must remove every trace of chemicals.

30 minutes.

Then I unscrew the lid and gently lift the spiral out. The film twists over its spool, and its moist surface is already beginning to show an intricate pattern in grey and black, matt and shiny. Taking care not to leave any fingerprints, I let the film unravel and hang it up to dry.

*

There are handprints left here and there in this house too. Ninety years ago, men's large hands left their marks at joins and behind panelling where they thought it wouldn't show. A few hours ago, Gupta finally agreed to come up to the attic with me. He had a bad conscience because the visit to the Theosophical archive had been postponed several times, and he wasn't "certain when it might take place".

We made our way together among the piles of rubbish until we reached a small, dusty door. According to Gupta, it led to what had been "a dark room at the time of Mrs Besant". He sighed and brushed vaguely at the dust, filling the air with fluff.

The room was very small, and nothing was left of the original fittings, Gupta explained. "Mrs Besant insisted on taking in the indigent from the East End during both world wars. In 1915, German airships threatened London, and then there was of course the bombing during the Blitz. Especially women and children from the slums without other support were given beds wherever there was a usable space. Up here, they kept prams and other salvaged possessions. Mementoes, mostly, that the women had rescued. Lansdowne Road was far enough from the river and the worst of the destruction to be reasonably safe, but the women could still get here on foot from the burning blocks in the East End."

It was still possible to see remnants of these wartime occupations: partitions taken down and plenty of grey paint – "containing arsenic to kill the lice". By now, Gupta was mumbling through a handkerchief pressed to his nose and mouth.

*

Gupta kept himself to himself and earnestly studied the rafters while I tried to push a box out of our way. It was impossibly heavy, and so I opened it to remove some of the contents. Most of them were old books and piles of tidily folded children's clothing, heavy with damp. There was a tin toy too, a green-painted model of a cannon-boat called *Tsushima*, maybe from around 1910. The books seemed too classy to have come from working-class homes in the East End. There were two mouldy but expensively leather-bound volumes on *Ancient Legends, Mystic Charms and Superstitions of Ireland* by someone mysteriously called Speranza.

The wall looked several shades darker behind the box, as if the wartime painters had not been bothered to move it. Even in the feeble light, the splattered marks were easy to see. They reflected light, like salt crystals on a wintry street or spilt drops of fixative under a darkroom light.

There were also small, blurred handprints made by children. I took several photos using my macro lens, moving in from about 3 feet to a few inches away, hoping to find a pattern later.

Gupta stayed around, watched me without comment.

*

A few hours later, I crawl into my narrow bed with a tumbler of amber whisky to keep me happy and the books on mystic legends from Ireland to keep me interested. Their covers shed flakes like old skin, and the stiff pages are difficult to separate. Around me, the old house creaks and groans like a ship in a storm. The cat has made a hollow at the bottom of my bed and curled itself into a warm, sleepy ball. Her heart ticks like a small timer. Now and then, she stretches her strong legs and twitches her whiskers as if dreaming some ancient feline dream of bloody hunts through the undergrowth.

Speranza – an unknown name to me – argues that in folk tales, elves were often conflated with the spirits of the dead, as if the two were one. The dead are always hovering near the living, and may be transformed into creatures like elves, some benign and some not at all. They might turn up suddenly to presage deaths or other serious events. The book tells of shape-changing, of magicians and witches turning into birds, horses, dogs or handsome young men in order to play tricks on slow-witted human beings. One of the spirits is young with white skin and a mane of flaming red hair. Shy of people, she walks alone over the moors. She watches over the old Irish families, and when a family member is close to death, she is glimpsed outside a window or open door. She has come to remind everyone in the house of their old sorrows, maybe of a baby born out of wedlock and secretly drowned in a bog-pool, or of the fading away of a young man or woman thwarted in love. Before switching off my bedside lamp, the last passage I read describes a female spirit called Banshee, from the Gaelic words *Bean Si*, or "Spirit of the Dead".

I put the book down, listening sleepily to the creaking and sighing of old, dry woodwork. The cat appraises me with eyes that gleam yellow in the lamplight, alert but unemotional. What she sees must bore her, because she yawns so widely that I can see her pink throat and sharp white teeth. Then we both go to sleep. I sleep deeply, dreaming the kind of dreams you never remember.

Brighton

"NO, I'M HERE on my own today," Neil McGowan says in a voice that suggests I had no business asking in the first place. Still, he agrees to answer some of my questions.

Speranza was the pseudonym used by a woman also known as Francesca Elgee. She was actually Lady Jane Frances Wilde, an Irish patriot with a great fund of knowledge about Irish folk tales, Oscar Wilde's mother, and a friend of Maud Gonne and William Butler Yeats. She and Yeats together collected Irish stories and myths, creating a treasure trove that is crucial to Celtic identity.

Neil suggests that the book might have belonged to Annie Besant. A pause follows. He is withholding information, and for a moment I can hear his long nails scratching his beard. But – yes, he has it – Alice Frobisher's address in Brighton. Number 10, Seaview Court. According to the city map, it's right on the seafront.

*

It's pouring with rain when I get off the train at Brighton. On the road, oily slicks suspended in water diffract the weak daylight to produce Pop-art effects. Hash-dream colours in patterns that shatter when I step on them.

In Queen's Road, the traffic roars though the greyness, dispersing the rain into a fine mist. I buy a coffee in the station, where the raw wind whistles through scaffolding. I sometimes wonder if every building in England is scheduled for refurbishment in time for the Millennium. It seems a particularly laborious way of controlling fear of the apocalypse, a kind of reassurance that rings hollow in a society that harbours hordes of homeless people, living and dying on the street. Many are addicts. Of course, it's no different back home. It's just that we behave ourselves and don't speak about such things.

The coffee tastes of water and something burnt. I pour most of it out. No rubbish bins as usual, due to the IRA's habit of planting bombs in them. Even though their politics seem much more decent and collaborative now, bins are still scarce. I leave the paper cup on the pavement with a deep sense of Swedish guilt.

"BIG ISSUE!" The magazine seller looks like a wild warrior, hairy and bearded, burnt by the sun and wearing amulets, shells, bits of bone and pierced flint on dirty leather straps round his neck. I read last night that elves and spirits can be seen through holes in stones. Maybe I should wear one.

It's just past 10 a.m. In half an hour, I'm due at Alice Frobisher's last home. I follow the traffic crawling towards the harbour. The ceaseless drizzle spatters everything, bouncing off metal and tarmac. My trainers are soaked through and wheeze with every step.

Halfway to the seafront, a small park – no more than a fenced lawn fringed with trees – has become a haven for the homeless. All kinds of people are sheltering from the cold rain in ramshackle constructions of plastic sheeting and cardboard. Ragged, worn-looking men and women are packed into a tight circle on the wet grass, surrounded by their dogs and bundles. There are at least ten of them, too many for the police to disperse. I half expect to see a plume of smoke from a sour campfire rising through the branches. Impossible, since it's forbidden to light fires in the park.

I turn into a side street, and the grinding traffic noises slowly die away. I pass the dark, cavernous back entrances of gambling arcades. Inside one of these grottoes, a fat woman is mopping the floor. Next, I'm watching two men wearing black caps hauling a defunct gambling machine into the back of a van. It says *DEATH WARRIOR* in red letters across the broken glass. The sun is back-lighting the lifting rain clouds, making it hard to see clearly as I follow a zigzag course along narrow streets to the harbour.

Seaview Court is a small, white-painted house close to the old, tumbledown West Pier. I'm a little early and walk down to the shingle. The Pier is a no-go area with a *DANGER KEEP OUT* sign nailed across the entrance and the wooden bridge removed, just in case. A double colonnade of rusty cast-iron pillars marching out into the choppy water is all that's left. Above, the gulls float in tight circles round the turrets, reminding me of the vultures I photographed once at the Tower of Silence on Malabar Hill outside Bombay. The decaying Pier looks like a pile of dirty-white birds' droppings or maybe Miss Havisham's mouldering wedding-cake, left to moulder on its dish for more than fifty years. On the way back, I come upon a placard, carefully taken down and hidden in the damp darkness underneath the Pier, which says that it was inaugurated in 1866 and was considered by the Victorians to be an architectural masterpiece. It is in the process of being restored.

*

When I finally knock on the door to number 10, the girl who opens it looks at me indifferently, moving lazily out of my way as I squeeze by her. She says her name is Suzah and spells it to make sure I get it right. Suzah has a ring in her nose, and when she opens her mouth, I notice that her tongue is pierced too. Her head is shaved, and her strongest feature is the kohl, black as soot, around her eyes, which makes her look like a silent-film actress. She is wearing a short lilac top and a pair of excessively tight jeans dyed saffron. She has put on black nail-varnish, and one of her stubby hands holds a well-thumbed Mervyn Peake paperback while the other clutches a buttered roll.

The house is as compact as a lighthouse. At first, it seems to consist only of a narrow, white-painted staircase with small pictures along the wall. Most of them are light, pretty watercolours with strong accents here and there, the red of poppies in a field or the deep blue of the sea.

As we climb the stairs, Suzah explains that her name used to be

Susan, but she has "like, left that stuff behind". She has been doing this museum job for a year. It's a work placement because she's registered as unemployed. Once I tell her that I'm a photographer, she chats easily, no longer seeming withdrawn.

"Photography sounds great, I'd love to do it," she says. "It makes you develop as a person, or somethin'."

"It can happen," I agree cautiously and then ask about Alice Frobisher.

*

None of Alice's big non-figurative paintings are left in the house. They are from a later period, when pattern and colour interested her more than anything else. After Max Frobisher's death in the 1920s, she got to know Vanessa Bell and others working in the Omega Workshop. Their new way of seeing influenced her and many other artists living on this coast. The play of light on the chalk cliffs and sea fascinated them.

The lady I spoke to on the phone, Miss Black, won't arrive until noon, and Suzah leaves me to explore on my own. Neatly written cards in each room tell of events in Alice's life. Otherwise, the house is empty apart from the paintings.

There is an octagonal room at the top, housed in a turret and with windows in every wall. The sun has come out, filling the room with light that makes it look blindingly white at first. I walk across the creaking floorboards, solid planks from the early years of the twentieth century, when the house was built. This was Alice's studio from the time she moved to Brighton in the 1930s. Her portable easel is still here, and a worn mackintosh, bleached to the colour of sand, hangs in a corner. I think it would crackle if I touched it. I observe the Pier, its outline black against the shining sea and divided into sections by the leaded windows.

A display cabinet is filled with pictures. One shows Alice and Max on the beach. She is wearing a slightly baggy '20s-style beach-dress and a white beret. His floppy straw hat is pulled well down over his forehead, shading most of his face. He is very thin, the white suit hanging loosely on his bony frame as if on a clothes-hanger. The photo is carefully annotated in fading ink. The time was July 1924 and the place Dieppe, only 10 or 15 miles from the Somme and the fields of Flanders.

The later snaps were taken with a Kodak Brownie displayed next to a group of pictures of Alice. In one from a visit to Dundalk in Ireland during October 1937, she stands in a bleak, rocky landscape wearing a dull-looking suit and smiling even though she is obviously cold.

I observe the room carefully. There are still stains on the floorboards where thick oil paint worked its way into cracks. The colours looks oddly fresh against the dark wood. Alice's absence can be felt as an emptiness typical of places where someone has lived for a long time and then left for good.

It's so quiet that I can hear the light scratching of feet on the roof and wonder if there is a colony of gulls living up there.

*

The sunlight feels burning hot on my back as I trundle uphill to the station. When I pass the homeless people's park, there's nobody around. The muddy, dishevelled lawn and a few sheets of cardboard, presumably too wet to recycle as building material, are the only signs of occupation. The traffic is heavier now, queues of solitary men revving their engines. My eyes are filling with fine grit. A cyclist weaves in and out among the cars. He is kitted out in a shiny black helmet, dark goggles and a mask. Apparently, exhaust fumes are turning the chalk cliffs yellow. I've been smoking too much, as usual, and the foul air seems to reach only halfway down into my lungs. By the time the station comes into view, I'm panting heavily. Some Japanese tourists block my way. They giggle shrilly as if at an unending joke.

Emperor Hirohito, the Son of the Sun, is going to visit London this summer. I recall images of British soldiers freed from Japanese prison camps, their bodies so frail – skeletons tightly covered by pale skin, thin as rice-paper. These are among the more repulsive of the photos in London's Imperial War Museum, a place that smells odd, maybe of gas, dried blood or mud. It is as if the remainders of war – torn uniforms, gas-masks, letters that were never sent – have generated a composite smell as distinct as a unit of measurement.

*

Once on the train, I sink back into the comfortable seat. Electronically controlled doors close soundlessly as I try to collect my thoughts about meeting Miss Black. It was quite a confusing experience.

At 79, Myrtle Black is still a beauty. She was born in the northern Indian town of Darjeeling in 1919. She told me a little about her life as we drank sweet, hot tea in a small room set aside for museum staff. Suzah was there too, and she put her book down to listen while sipping her tea. Myrtle is a small, slender woman with a very straight back. Her face is as pale and finely drawn as the yellowing cameo at the neck of her lightly starched white blouse. Her language too reminded me of that carved image, a little old-fashioned and exquisitely precise.

*

Myrtle's parents owned a tea plantation called Blackleaves in Sikkim, a small province situated in the foothills of the huge mountains of Nepal and Bhutan near the Indian border. The plantation had been named after the family's decaying estate in Ireland. The two-storey house was built of reddish wood that smelled of resin. The planta-tion was at too high an altitude to prosper, and in 1924 frost destroyed almost the entire crop. The Indian pickers whispered to each other that this was because of the bad-luck name Blackleaves, but only Myrtle listened to them. The plantation went bankrupt, the Blacks managing to hold on to just enough money to pay for their passage back to England in 1925. One year later, Mr and Mrs Black died, as anonymously as they had lived, in a train accident near Slough.

Myrtle was then seven years old, spoiled by her parents and, espe-cially, by her Indian nanny. After her parents' death, she was cared for by an unmarried aunt who ran a "simple but clean and proper" boarding house in Brighton. This lady, who was unused to children and whose heart had been weakened by the Spanish flu a few years earlier, turned out to be a much better parent than one might have thought. She earned extra money by playing the piano at tea and evening dances at the Hotel Metropole, "a most elegant place". Myrtle, meanwhile, learned to look after herself.

In the summer of 1927, she met Alice and Max Frobisher for the first time.

*

Between the wars, the West Pier was considered *the* place for polite society to take the air – "not at all like that vulgar Palace Pier nowadays". The wide, silvery floors would creak slightly as the waves slammed against the wrought-iron pillars, and the feeling of being on board a great ship was enhanced by a large, shining, white lifeboat hanging from pulleys. It was there, ready to go, should someone fall in or – for it seemed possible – should the whole Pier slip its moorings and float away. High above the glazed arches of the pavilions rose flagpoles flying pennants that flapped and snapped in the wind. There would be live music in the Rotunda, waltzes or the new jazz tunes. Al Jolson's *The Jazz Singer* had been shown at the Alhambra, and people loved it so much that they carried their wind-up gramophones to the Pier, playing "Sonny Boy" and "Mammy" over and over again. The rasping, rhythmic sounds would drift with the endlessly circling gulls out to sea, towards the blue horizon where coal smoke rose from the many ferries plying the waves between Britain and France and the rest of the Continent.

*

Myrtle's memory of the day she met the Frobishers is very lucid. It happened in the afternoon, she knows, because her shadow fell long and dark across the sun-heated boardwalk. She had brought her red leather ball to play with on the Pier, which was tricky but interesting because it could so easily end up in the water.

Buses brought lots of bathers from the station to the beach. The boys would dig for gold coins or try to catch crabs, and the girls would collect pebbles. Myrtle had found a lovely blue flint with a hole in so she could hang it on a string round her neck.

There was a constant, gentle background noise of splashing and rustling. Gentlemen would remove their ties, roll up their trousers and go wading, still wearing their waistcoats and white shirts. Now and then, a bigger wave would wet their trouser bottoms, and the gentlemen would stagger back towards land. Paddling about peacefully, they often tied drooping knots in the corners of their handkerchiefs and wore them as improvised sun-shades. This was new to Myrtle, who remembered colonial hard hats, sun-bleached khaki over cork.

Myrtle was playing with her ball when a boy came running past and kicked it hard. It flew over the railing and would have been lost had it not been for a tall, thin gentleman who caught it smartly, like a cricket ball. It was half-hidden inside his large hand when he doffed his wide-brimmed hat politely to her. The breeze pulled at the remaining strands of his hair, and his hands were covered in brown spots. His face was thin and pale, but looked kind.

The man said that his name was Max, and Myrtle told him her name, going on to tell him about the resin-scented house in Darjeeling and how the creaking noises of the Pier reminded her of it at the height of the monsoon. During the worst rains, it was almost as if the whole rickety place, veranda and all, might take off and fly away over the treetops. She added that she longed to go back to the brownish-red house in the hills. Max seemed to understand exactly how she felt.

Max said that he hadn't played cricket since Cambridge, back in 1894, but that he was pleased to see that he could still stop a ball when he had to. Then he told her how, that very afternoon, he had been to see an Indian magician called Nan Parjat Singh. Singh received people in his arcade premises near the beach. Max had walked by and gone inside on an impulse. The magician had read Max's palm, and the important thing was that he would meet somebody special later that day. Max and his wife, who was an artist, were in Brighton on holiday and staying in a B&B. Max's wife was working on a picture, and Max had to see a doctor, a specialist, every day at 1 p.m. Afterwards, he liked to stroll to the Pier.

They met every day for the rest of the summer.

Before she could go on, Myrtle had another drink of tea and sat quietly, her eyes downcast, for a while. She picked nervously at the hem of her grey cardigan, suddenly looking sad and lonely. Old.

*

Some visitors arrived, and Suzah reluctantly dragged herself away to show them around. There were steps and voices upstairs now, adding to the constant rumbling from the heavily trafficked coastal road outside.

I tried to imagine Brighton in the '20s, holiday-makers strolling easily in the sunshine, complete with walking sticks and white gloves, felt hats for the gentlemen and pudding-dish sun hats for the ladies. They would pay calls in the afternoons or attend tea dances. I could almost hear the shingle crunching under their feet and visualise the Hotel Metropole's striped awnings extended against the afternoon heat. Then I imagined the roaring traffic reduced to the engine noises of the odd car trundling past at a maximum speed of 30 miles per hour. But the image slipped away.

Myrtle had recovered her composure.

"It *is* hard to imagine it all, isn't it? What it was like, all those years ago. That is what you were thinking about, am I right?"

I nodded.

"I keep quite a few of Max's things here. I inherited a great deal, not the best pictures naturally, but a lot of things. I simply don't have enough room for everything at home. Max's gramophone records, for example. They're a great help for bringing memories back."

She rose a little stiffly and left the room. When she returned, she was carrying an old-fashioned gramophone with a handle. It was well looked after. A 78-rpm record was already in place on the turntable.

"He took me to my first real concert," she said. "Fritz Kreisler, the great violinist. He played at the Concert Society. I even know the date – August 22, 1927. 'Liebeslied'."

The sound was scratchy, claustrophobic, slightly spooky and terribly sentimental. I thought of all those who had listened then, dead and gone now. Many had been cheated of their lives, dying far too young in the war.

*

In the 1920s, it was tempting to idealise the pre-war past, when the world was safe – or so many wanted to believe. Their very conventionality, their gloves, uniforms and buttoned-up waist-coats, suggested a desire for a stable, cultured society. I had only begun to examine that past in pictures not meant for posterity and had found nothing particularly reassuring. Images trap us in mental frameworks. Take the attempted assassination in Sarajevo on June 28, 1914. Pictures from the Serbs' national day of celebration show the finery of the Archduke and his wife, pomp and circumstance and orderly behaviour. Images like these are a form of collective memory; they live on in people's minds, just as old saws do about the value of hard work or whatever. Maybe these are essential mechanisms to ensure the survival of human societies.

When the gramophone needle entered the final track, I asked Myrtle if Max or Alice had ever mentioned their adopted daughter, a girl called Dora. Before answering, she got up to move the gramophone arm gently back onto its rest.

"Yes. Alice and I went to Ireland together, to look both for my family and for the family of the girl – Dora. I was only 18 then, but Alice insisted that I go with her. In Max's place, I suppose. We managed to persuade my aunt somehow. The fact that we had already been given money by the Frobishers presumably wasn't unconnected with the granting of permission. I kept a diary throughout, and I recall the journey very clearly."

She sat down at the table again.

"Alice and Max had been sent a parcel many years earlier, around 1920 I think. They lived in Weymouth then, and Max was still reasonably fit. Alice hadn't told me about it, only she insisted that we go to a small village on the north-east coast, quite close to the Ulster border. It took time to get there; the roads were pretty bad, and Alice was not used to driving. So there was plenty of time to tell the story.

"Such an odd trip. It was pouring with rain, and the deep potholes had turned to pools. The car bumped and slithered all over the place. More than once, I thought I'd be sick. Drystone walls followed the road on both sides for mile after mile, up hill and down dale, melting into the grey sky on the crests of the hills. It was beyond me that so much stone could exist. These were ancient rocks, covered in white lichen, ridged like old bits of worn wood. The walls were carefully constructed, with gaps for the wind to blow through, but seemed always to have been there, as unchanging as the moorland and the yellowing, dripping grasses. It was a silly notion, of course, and I realised that people had actually built the walls, struggled and worked, fetched and carried for generations. I must have been affected by the emptiness of the landscape. We hardly saw a soul. That corner of the world seemed deserted. Maybe, I thought, the people there had been turned into stones and were hiding in the roadside ditches, watching us.

"Sheep were the only living creatures around in large numbers. There would be whole gangs of them standing in the road, dull and stubborn and massive in their thick, greasy coats, their eyes like yellow glass balls. Alice and I took turns to shoo them out of the way. The journey became so terrible that all we could do was laugh, but I suppose she felt that she owed me some sort of explanation.

"So she told me about the parcel. It had been carefully wrapped with brown paper and string, postmarked New York 1919 but with no details of the sender. Alice said that it must have been ages in transit and had got to look very tatty. The parcel contained a wallet or, better, a kind of purse. It was lockable, had many compartments and was made of stained, dark leather. Most of the compartments were empty, which is perhaps why Alice took such a long time to get round to investigating it carefully. Two initials, M. F., were rather crudely stamped into the leather. In the central pocket was a sailor's accreditation in the name of Michael Flaherty, stating that he was 'an experienced seaman, with some skills in reading and arithmetic'. The home address was Dundalk, Ireland. In 1905, Flaherty had left his ship in Whitby on the Yorkshire coast. A receipt announced that on June 10, 1905, Captain O'Leary had paid Mick Flaherty £20 owed in wages. Flaherty had signed clumsily with his initials. The pin holding the two sheets of paper together was rusty.

"There was no money in the wallet and only two other bits of paper. One was a blank postcard showing 'A View of New York Harbor'. It had been kept in one of the outer compartments and was marked with a nasty brown stain which still felt sticky. The other was a visiting card made of thick, expensive paper. The printed text said *Annie Besant, Nr 17, Lansdowne Road, London W11*. It was an odd thing for Mick Flaherty to have had, and it interested Alice most of all.

"When the last lot of sheep scampered off, bored with staring at us, we set out determined to reach Dundalk before the evening. By then I was feeling quite curious."

*

At the southern end of Battersea Park, I watch the three gasometers, half-hidden in hollows and looking like three grey, bulky old ladies. Closer to the river, Battersea Power Station rears up, an almost ruined, huge shell of a building – a colossal oven gone cold, its four grooved chimneys pointing towards the sky like cannons. As the train crosses the river near Chelsea Bridge, the sounds of it bumping over points bounce off the water far below. The setting sun is as brightly orange as my childhood memory of Cape oranges. It hovers just above the skyline of the blue city, its glowing surface marred by dark streaks of pollution.

As the train jerks along, switching slowly among the many tracks leading into Victoria Station, I close my eyes and recall the end of Myrtle's story. It makes the last fragments of broken bone fit together.

Dundalk: 1937

"WE ARRIVED IN Dundalk at dusk. It had just stopped raining, and the air felt very clean and fresh, as if it had been washed like the big sheets hung out to dry on lines next to the village shop. The shop was in a white two-storey house, which also served as an inn. Alice had booked a room for the night. She had also sent a letter explaining our mission to the priest in Dundalk.

"There was no point in doing anything that evening. We were tired, and it was quickly becoming dark. We had hot mutton pie, home-baked bread and pints of the local dark bitter. While we ate, Alice spoke of Dora and of her own friendship with Annie Besant. Later that evening, she told me an old Irish folk tale about a King who could change into animals. He very much liked turning into a nightingale, because they sing more beautifully than any other bird. Then, one evening, his wife thoughtlessly made a dreadful mistake that broke the spell, instead condemning the King and his most faithful henchmen to sleep deep inside a mountain. They were to stay there until the end of time, when the King would ride out in front of his men, and together they would save Ireland.

"Alice fell silent. Just at that moment, a glowing coal crashed hissing through the fire. We both jumped, burst out laughing and couldn't stop. The landlord popped his head round the door after a while. He must've thought that the hardships of travelling had made us crazy.

*

"Autumn had emptied the inn at Dundalk of visitors, though quite a few would come in the summer, including Englishmen who liked the fishing. The clean, pleasant bedrooms were on the second floor. The beds seemed soft and cosy, though slightly damp. That first night, we were both exhausted, and I slept deeply until the seabirds started crying well before dawn.

"The day started clear and sunny, but the air was chilled by a stiff wind. The views seemed to stretch for miles, both out over the sea at Dundalk Bay and northwards, towards the border with Northern Ireland. The Mourne hills rose in a crown of blue and violet peaks over the brown heaths.

"Dundalk was little more than ten or so houses strung out at odd angles along one road like wild berries threaded on to a straw. The road ran steeply down towards the sea. Still, it had a post office as well as the inn-cum-shop. The shop sold a range of useful things – Horniman's tea, Bovril, shiny oilskins, ropes, whetting steel, thin butcher's knives and rubber boots. We both bought boots and thick woollen socks. The ground had dried a little, but the sunlight was feeble, and once you left the village, the mud squelched underfoot.

"The priest, Father Martin Sander, walked with us the short distance to the church. It stood on a grassy hillock outside the village, over-looking the bay and the Irish Sea beyond. Uneven rows of cracked and weathered gravestones guarded the stout medieval edifice, which had been built from slabs of grey stone. It seemed grown out of the rock, up there only thinly covered with soil. The wind felt stronger, and out to sea it was already driving rows of white-crested waves.

"Father Sander was middle-aged, short and tough with the weather-beaten face of a fisherman or farmer. Quiet and authoritative, he led the way to Mick Flaherty's grave. It was overgrown with grass, and the stone was leaning over. Alice and the priest both bent down to push the grass away. The sun was disappearing quickly behind a leaden bank of clouds, and I got very cold. I was standing with my back to the wind, wearing a thick duffel coat that Alice had bought for me in Dublin, but the chill cut through the thick material. I watched people on the beach collecting seaweed into big baskets. A bit further along, a fire of peat and driftwood was burning.

"Father Sander came over to speak to me. His cassock smelled of mould and cured fish.

"'The boys started the fire to cook the mussels coming up with the seaweed. I don't know, it may be unhealthy, but it's food when all's said and done. A poor place, this is . . . but we stick together and help each other out.'

"For a while, I stood watching the sour smoke tossed about by gusts of wind, feeling that I could almost smell the heady scents of burning peat and wet wood. Then I thought about the bog-men found here and there, wonderfully well-preserved bodies that had been buried for hundreds of years under layers of peat. Having usually been killed quickly by being strangled or having their throats cut, their stomach contents of porridge and herbs would still be intact. The scene on the beach shifted slowly as people came and went between the seaweed gathering and the warm fire. Their dark coats flapped in the wind.

"When Alice had cleared the grass and lichen off the gravestone, the first inscription could be seen: *Moira Fianna Flaherty Born in Dundalk 1872. Died in the arms of the Lord on the 3rd January 1902.* Beneath it was *Michael Sinn Flaherty *1869 †1905.*

"'Flaherty belonged to one of the old families of Ireland,' said Father Sander. 'His people came from Galway and had their origins way back in the time of the legends. Mick Flaherty was restless, that he was. He left when his wife died, took to the road and was gone. He was not liked in the village, people thought him a stranger – an incomer. They tell me his looks too were different from people here. I don't know what happened to his children. Dora and Tom they were called. Dora was the older one, born in 1892. Tom was two years younger. My pre-decessor recorded them as "Moved from this Parish". He for one didn't like Mick Flaherty and was known to call him a "notorious heathen".'

"The wind had risen. The rain started up, and we slithered down the narrow, grassy path to the rectory. It stood halfway between the church and the village – 'both inside the community and separate from it', as the priest put it. Near the house, he had managed to grow a wild privet hedge as protection from the harsh, salt-laden wind. Slender branches were slapping against the house, and Sander waved us indoors while he stayed behind to tie them back in place. Bending over against the wind, we fought our way round the corner to the heavy, green-painted front door kept closed with an ancient iron latch.

"Inside was a small lobby with a bench along the wall. Next to it was a collection of fishing gear. Single hooks and sets, lines, weights and a long knife with the priest's initials carved in the handle had all been thrown into a large bucket. Pinkish water had collected in its buckled bottom, and a few scales were floating in it. Next to the bucket was a sack full of coarse salt and a rag stiff with dried blood. A sharp smell of fish hung in the air.

"The priest was smiling when he came in a few minutes later, though his cassock was dripping wet and his face was reddened by the cold. It seemed that the wind and rain had put him in a good mood. Leading the way into the sitting room, he installed us on the sofa. The room was low-ceilinged, dark and lined with books. Their leather-bound spines somehow absorbed the feeble light entering through the narrow windows. Not even the pervasive fish odour could hide the faint, sickly smell of mould.

"Father Sander served us hot, strong tea and, smiling cheerfully, added a large shot of Irish whiskey to each of the cups. He looked contentedly at the books.

"'I have the habit of going to Dublin once a month, God willing and the weather as well. My happiest time is spent browsing in anti-quarian bookshops, looking for volumes of Irish history, archaeology and suchlike. Real interests of mine, all that. But the house is damp, and it affects my books.'

"He leaned back, sipping his tea. Putting the cup down, he rubbed his cold-looking, red hands on his knees in what seemed a habitual gesture. His hands were stubby and strong. There was a half-healed cut on one index finger. While Alice drank a cautious mouthful of powerful tea, Sander noticed my curious look.

"'St Peter was a fisherman too,' he said in a teasing voice. Then he turned to Alice.

"'Michael Flaherty was shipped back home in his coffin. That was in the spring of 1906. We didn't open the coffin, because his identity had already been established back in London. An anonymous benefactor paid for everything – transport, funeral and burial expenses, including the mason who cut the inscription on the stone. Since no-one round here cared at all if Moira's man was alive or dead, it was just as well that the money was forthcoming. If not, Flaherty would've ended up in a pauper's grave in London, like as not. That's where he was murdered, of course. As a matter of fact, that murder investigation is quite a story. For a start, it was the first time a corpse was identified from a photograph. My predecessor was mighty interested in the proceedings and collected newspaper articles and suchlike. He even approached the Chief of Police in Dublin and got him to send extracts from the police records. They found Flaherty's body in the East End, by the Millwall Tap Brewery. Let me see now. I got all the documents ready after I received your letter.'

"He rose and went over to a desk under the windows where he began shifting papers about, stirring up a large cloud of dust into the already murky air. After a while, he returned with a slim bundle of yellowing cuttings and official-looking documents.

"'Look at this headline. It's a cutting from the *Daily Telegraph* dated August 12, 1905. "UNKNOWN MAN FOUND DEAD NEAR MILL-WALL DOCKS."'

"Sander unfolded the brittle paper. At the bottom of the page, a stylish advertisement informed readers that 'The Right Colours for this Season Are Havana Brown, Napoléon Blue, Mahogany, Squirrel Grey, Forester Green and Amethyst.' The old priest had put a cross in the margin next to the article that described how the corpse had been found, and Father Sander leaned forward, reading as his finger followed the lines. The smell of fish seemed to become more intense.

EAST LONDON A worker in the Millwall Brewery yesterday made a most unpleasant and macabre discovery on the quayside. Behind a few barrels, stacked in readiness for cleaning, he found the body of a man of about 40 years of age. The corpse was strongly built, but in too a bad a condition for more detailed appraisal. The man had been wearing simple workman's clothing, to wit a brown woollen jacket, a white collarless shirt, black, slightly too short trousers and brown, somewhat worn boots. No other belongings were found. The man had died following a knifing that slit open his abdomen. Police constables from the Metropolitan Police were called out and joined by members of the Harbour Police Force. A thorough investigation was carried out, both of the body and the place where it had been found. The authorities are still not prepared to release any further details concerning this event, but cannot exclude the possibility that the man was dead before being transported to the Millwall site.

"Sander went on reading aloud to us from the papers in the bundle. The crime had attracted public attention for exactly two weeks, which was quite a long time given that the victim was a working-class man. One particular detail had confused the police and kept newspaper readers intrigued. The autopsy revealed that the corpse's mouth and throat contained half-chewed, sticky, dark green leaves. It seemed that the man had been about to swallow at the moment of his death. There was no plant material in his stomach. The membranes inside his mouth, his tongue and teeth were coloured a vivid red, not from blood but from a red fluid of plant origin. The old, chewed leaves gave off a harsh, rather disgusting smell.

"After washing off the dead man's saliva, a botanist was persuaded to attempt an identification of the ovate leaves. He pronounced the specimen to be from a plant called *Digitalis purpurea*. *Digitalis* grows wild all over the British Isles; its common name is purple foxglove.

An ethnologist called Dr A. H. Burton wrote an article in *The Times* about the magic qualities ascribed to this plant and the use of its properties in folk medicine. He stated that the name *foxglove* is a distortion of the old *folk's glove,* reflecting the belief that the slender flower-tubes were the gloves of elves.

"A juice with a characteristic smell can be extracted from foxglove leaves which, properly prepared, strengthens the heartbeat. In its raw form it is a dangerous poison that slows the heart, and hence the circulation, dramatically. The net effect is that of strangulation. The reduced oxygen supply to the brain leads first to a state resembling intoxication and then to death.

"Identifying the corpse was more difficult. Scotland Yard had no record of his fingerprints. Francis Galton, working in India in the 1890s, had perfected the technique of fingerprinting using black printer's ink and had gone on to collect and classify fingerprints according to three fundamental types showing whorls, curves and arches. In India, important documentation, such as wills and contracts, have since ancient times been confirmed by a hand- or a foot-print, originally in clay or on thin hides, and later on paper. The fingerprints of our corpse were of no help in identifying him, however.

"House-to-house inquiries in the Mile End Road tenements proved fruitless, and extending the search to working-men's hostels in Limehouse and Poplar and then to East End Salvation Army hostels didn't help either. Finally, the priest in the Irish seamen's church identified the man as Michael Flaherty. By then, the peace treaty between Japan and Russia had taken over the headlines. From August 29, when the treaty was signed in Portsmouth, Mick Flaherty was forgotten.

"Sander put down the cutting, looking at us while he folded it carefully. His eyes were brown and a little bloodshot.

"'The foxglove, now. It grows freely, like a weed, all over grassland in these parts. It doesn't mind stony ground and salty wind. I've got several cultivars in my own garden. Round here at least, it's been used as a medicinal herb for perhaps a thousand years. If you dry the leaves and keep them away from light, they stay potent for months.'

"He rose and disappeared into the kitchen, where we could hear him rummaging for something. It turned out to be a black-glazed stoneware jar with a wooden lid. Opening it, he pulled out a handful of crumbled dried leaves which he rubbed between his fingers before holding out his hand for us to smell. We both backed away from the odour, bitter and harsh but at the same time rich and nauseating.

"'There you are, *Digitalis purpurea*, harvested from my own garden some two years ago,' the priest said, sniffing the dark flakes before pouring them back into the jar.

"'Now, Flaherty's leaves were fresh, and they could've come from a garden or, indeed, from any bit of open ground in London. By the way, we do know quite a lot about how Flaherty got to the city, mostly due to a young policeman anxious to put himself forward as a promising detective. Mick worked his way to London by taking jobs in forestry and gardening. He moved fairly often, but doesn't seem to have had any problems finding work. Large estates were more common then, and he was apparently especially good with animals. He seems to have kept himself to himself, and when he did travel, he went at quite a speed, presumably hurrying to find his children.'

*

"We left Sander soon afterwards. The rain had stopped, and the sun appeared in fitful glimpses from behind scurrying clouds, creating a pattern of dark and light across the fields and uplands. Out at sea, another bank of clouds was becoming so dense that it seemed to rest on the water, blotting out the horizon.

"On the way back to the inn, Alice and I were quiet. I realised that she must be thinking about Dora and all these events from long ago, never fully explained or put to rest.

"After the evening meal, I knew that it would be impossible to sleep unless I took a walk. I went out alone in the gathering dusk. The rain had changed into drizzle, and drops were stirring the tidal pools. The high tide was due, and soon the beach would become the bottom of the sea. Walking down the path to the beach, I saw a little boy playing alone, poking around in the waterlogged ashes of the fire. When I came closer, I realised that he wasn't more than 5 or 6 years old. Even so, he seemed to feel the hostility to strangers that was the norm in Dundalk.

"'Ma mum says you're snoopin,' he said, looking carefully at me. He thought for a while. 'Mum says you've no business here,' he added, rather more loudly.

"I wanted to get away from him and started off along the beach. The sand shifted under my feet.

"'Mum says for you to go away,' he shouted shrilly before running off towards the village. Wondering if he understood what he was saying, I told myself that he was just echoing the talk of grown-ups.

"I came across another path leading up from the beach. The drizzle was becoming rain again. The sky and the land were a uniform dark grey, and the cries of the seabirds were coming from just above the surface of the sea. Ahead of me, a flock of gulls was foraging for food in the grass, attracting worms by drumming on the ground with seemingly deliberate cunning. The big birds hardly noticed me. It was late in the year; the time for hunting would soon be over, and the time to put on body fat had come.

"The path took me to the far side of the village, to a ruined house that I hadn't noticed before. The ruins must have been exposed to weather and wind for a long time. Very little was left apart from a chimney-breast that pointed into the air like a blackened, crooked finger, as if to sense the direction of the wind.

"The autumn downpours had flattened the grass into a fibrous mat like a troll's hair, covering the roughly dressed stones. The fireplace was a black hole surrounded by cracks and streaks of soot. Where the doorway had once been, a large flagstone was laid on the ground. It might have been taken from some burial mound up in the hills. Here it had become the place where you kicked off your muddy boots before going inside or where you put dishes of warm milk or beer out for the elves to drink.

"I explored for a little while in the stiffening wind and found a hand-made iron door-hinge and an iron cauldron, almost disintegrated from rust. The wind was cold and fierce enough to take my breath away, and the darkness had become almost total. I knew I had to return to the village.

*

"The way down was harder to negotiate. Below me, the sea was on its way in over the beach, leaving only a narrow dry margin to walk on. Between the ruin and the village was a deep ravine, which looked likely to fill with water because its rocky faces were free of grass. I had to go by the beach. Trying anything else would take time and could be dangerous. As I slowly edged downwards, bent against the wind, I wondered who might have lived in the ruined house. A wise woman? A witch? Or perhaps that strange man known as Michael Sinn Flaherty from Galway?

"The tide was being pushed inland by the strong wind, and as I clambered up to higher ground, the rushing green water was at my heels.

*

"Next morning, we set out early in order to get back to Dublin. Sleep had been almost impossible, because the wind had made the shutters bang and crash all night. I thought I'd heard birds screaming too. When the morning came with stillness and fitful sunshine, we were both very tired.

"We carried our suitcases to the mud-spattered car, and Alice unlocked the boot. It was a black Rover with lots of room for luggage, as I recall. Anyway, there was a dead bird in the boot. Its thin neck had been broken. We could not understand how it had got in. Alice gently lifted the frail body, saying she'd seen similar birds in Weymouth and that she thought it was a lark particular to the coast. In the end, we put it back in the car after stowing our things and closed the boot quietly. We drove off feeling rather frightened.

−134−

"Alice wanted to go inland to look for the Black family estate, which was supposed to be somewhere in the forest north of Dublin. We tried hard to find it, driving for hours on twisting, potholed roads lined with hedges that made them into dark, leafy tunnels. We followed the River Boyne, crawling over tiny, ancient bridges across stony streams and along canals with slow-flowing water the colour of beer. All the time we asked people for directions, but nobody seemed to know of the place. We never found it. We were probably just going round in circles by taking these narrow gravel roads in every possible direction, but it seemed as if the greenery, all that ivy and the succulent verdigris-green mosses, had simply crawled all over the house and engulfed it. My family had left more than fifty years earlier, and I somehow didn't feel that this was my country. We decided to give up.

"As we drove, Alice spoke about Mick Flaherty and his wife. She was sure that they had been driven out of the village and that hatred of them was part of local tradition. That everyone's righteous grand-parents had hated the Flahertys made it right to continue to do so. People were like that, she argued, not evil in themselves but ever anxious to do things the proper, accepted way. Keeping their outlook on life tidy, like an unused, chilly drawing room."

*

My train pulls into Victoria Station just as the digital display shows 18:00. People are already racing across the large concourse to reach the vacated carriages. Seconds earlier, the information display had been clicking, the stacks of discs rotating like counters in a game-machine and then settling to show destinations and platform numbers. I push against the oncoming crowds, elbows out. It takes me ten minutes to get out of the station, and when I stop on the pavement, I feel hungry and worn out.

A man standing on a red plastic pallet next to the entrance to the Tube station is giving an impromptu political speech, questioning the reality behind images.

"Images rule us," he shouts. "We believe what they seem to show us, competent politicians, democratically elected and determined men and women, *but* . . . *real* power is hidden behind images. Power lies within complicated networks that shuffle money across the globe, way beyond control by the people. Images distract us! They make it possible to cheat us. It's like a huge stage-set, a film full of tricks . . ."

His voice sounds hoarse and tired. It fades as I descend into the echoing corridors leading to the trains. I pass a thin man with long, filthy hair playing Brahms' violin concerto with inexpressible pain.

Dinner with Mr Gupta
(and Something about Gardens)

WHEN I ARRIVE back home, there are two lighted lamps with red paper shades hanging outside Gupta's door. Their flickering makes my shadow split and dance on the basement wall. Inside, I'm greeted by a rich, warm smell of roasted chicken spiced with saffron and curry, and mingling with the fainter scent of flamed spirits.

Gupta, a little sweaty from the kitchen, materialises like a plump Oriental Spirit of Food.

"Please, do me the honour to enter," he says genteelly.

He has laid on a dinner for his older brother Nat, his sister Rea and her daughter Siralee. The occasion is Siralee's 29th birthday. The food is plentiful and very good – "spiced with last year's harvest of herbs". There is red wine and port with the coffee. The pudding is a dish of pears, simmered to golden tenderness in French brandy.

Although I want to keep my distance, I can't help becoming chatty, even sentimental, after the third glass of wine. I speak of family life and togetherness, which is something I've actually never experienced. My parents divorced in 1961 and haven't spoken to each other since. Even when they did talk, their conversation ran through me like long, radiating cracks filled with hatred. No point in telling the Guptas about all that. When Rea asks me why I'm unmarried and childless, I quickly change the subject to the Gupta family home. Nat, Rea and "young" Siralee share a small terraced house at the top of Lonsdale Road in Notting Hill.

"Five rooms, but tiny. And the kitchen drain is blocked at present, so we came here instead."

The older Guptas share the odd habit of stressing certain words, which gives the most ordinary statements a kind of authority. Siralee speaks quietly and unemphatically, but very, very clearly. She is taking a post-graduate degree in biology at University College and hides behind square spectacles with heavy frames. With her thin, angular body and small, mobile, but cold hands, she reminds me of a monkey – perhaps one of the greedy, long-tailed little creatures which keep such vigilant watch over the graves in Bombay. This is meant to be her night, and everyone is trying hard to make her the focus of attention. She certainly eats more than anyone else, but between mouthfuls she often and rather pedantically corrects her older relatives' grammar.

We speak of India, in particular the north-western provinces. The older Guptas were born in a small village near the border with Pakistan. They describe the very large, old baobab tree in the marketplace, with its sticky, cucumber-like fruits known as monkey-bread. The birds used to rest within its vast canopy during the midday heat, and the fruits attracted swarms of insects during the night. The baobab's smell is curiously stale, and you can pull its soft, porous bark apart with your hands.

Nat, Rea and P. V. cannot remember much more about their old home. They were all "very small" in 1946, when the family decided to "accept the long-standing – indeed, more than one hundred years old – imperial invitation to move to Great Britain". Rea married an Englishman, an Army officer, who unfortunately stepped on a land-mine during a tour in Belfast in 1971. Since then Rea and her daughter have been staying with Nat. P. V. and their old parents lived there too until the senior Guptas died of high old age.

Gupta furnished his flat mainly with pieces from the Lansdowne Road house, but also with things donated by his family. The candle flames cast their still light over the objects in the hot, airless room. The most striking ornament is a dancing Shiva carved from a single block of shiny black wood. Parental portraits stare down at us with faces suggesting disapproval. They hang above a low bookshelf with a number of Theosophical works about Flowing Life Energies and the Aura by Annie Besant and Charles Leadbeater, thick volumes of Mme Blavatsky's collected thoughts and a Bible. Reassuringly, there is also a big book about gardening and a handful of much-read thrillers by writers like Dorothy Sayers, John Dickson Carr and Mickey Spillane. While I'm scanning the book titles, Siralee sidles up. She is polishing her glasses on one of the linen napkins. Exposed, her large eyes look slightly fearful. Once more, I think of a small, alert animal.

"It's so hot in here," she announces in her low, unexpectedly decisive voice. I nod, waiting for more, but she remains silent. Behind us, Nat, Rea and Gupta are reminiscing noisily.

"I wouldn't mind some fresh air," I say, meaning it.

We have to walk through both of Gupta's rooms to get to the garden door. I had seen the garden as a green wilderness outside the windows, but never found the way out. The path is narrow and winds its way among various obstacles lurking in the darkness, but Siralee has remembered to bring a torch. The cat decided to join us, following like a shadow. It is so quiet in the cool air under the trees that it is hard to believe that we are in the centre of London.

Without hesitating, Siralee takes my hand and we wander off deeper into the garden.

Gardens have been with us since ancient Egypt. At the time of the Pharaohs, two thousand years before Christ, they signified the annexation of land. Wealthy, cultured people set aside land for their own needs, taming wild and erratic nature. Horticulture differed from agriculture, for gardening was seen as an art and the emphasis was on Culture, though not to the exclusion of useful fruits and herbs. Rigorously planned gardens seem symptomatic of hierarchical, feudal systems – states in which high taxes, political oppression and religious bigotry dominated. English parkland suggests a gentler model. It is just as "unnatural" as its stricter German or French counterparts, but the layout is deceptively natural, hiding many features from the casual observer. The design is based on elements of light and shade, on sudden vistas, new perspectives and visual surprises. These archetypal English gardens from the eighteenth and nineteenth centuries revel in grottoes and secrets, playing with the new sense of being able to control Nature. By then, the natural sciences were providing laws and schemata that appeared to reduce Nature's dangers, and it no longer stood for the unexplored. The garden encroached ever deeper into the land outside. It was seen as a representation of Nature, as a slice of the wilderness and as dark and damp and full of secret corners into which not even the scientist could find his way. This myth of the garden was dominant for another century. Nature was an unpredictable, indeed a feminine, being, but women were not allowed to become architects and creators of decorative gardens until the late nineteenth and early twentieth centuries. These had been the province of well-to-do men for thousands of years, while women had been very welcome to work hard in the fields and vegetable plots. Thus it was that Gertrude Jekyll (1843–1932) began collaborating with the Arts and Crafts architect Edwin Lutyens, with whom she designed "natural" gardens in a symbiotic relationship with houses – a marriage of Nature and Culture.

It is a large garden, almost a park. Now and then, Siralee stops to point out places of special significance. She has discovered areas planted with bulbs or almost overgrown roses or hidden bits of paving. She describes the borders where Annie Besant cultivated roses, now growing wild, and how a little weeding would uncover the rich, friable soil. We walk across a lawn made thick and bouncy by invading mosses and tough grasses. The trees form dense black masses, their long-established root systems pushing like gripping fingers into the ground. A glassless glasshouse leans against a wall, an overgrown herb garden with bushy mints and lavenders waits for the care it needs to spring back to life. Siralee can't resist pulling at the suffocating layers of grass.

It occurs to me that Annie Besant might have cultivated foxgloves or, alternatively, that these versatile plants might have grown wild somewhere in the garden. Stopping under the trees, I light a cigarette while I look back at the house, dark apart from the light in the basement windows. Siralee's party is still in full swing.

The ground smells of damp and life and rot. I pick up one of last year's leaves. My eyes must have got used to the low light level because I can see the fragile network of veins, evidence of a shape that has all but vanished.

There is a small fountain, green with verdigris, in the middle of the lawn. A statuette of a slender female form stands on a rickety base at its centre. Her face is covered with a greenish bronze veil, as if she is in mourning. It comes to me that the figure is *The Spirit of Nature*, the best-known piece by a long-forgotten artist. The angle of the base makes the statue seem ready to leap over the edge, more daring than mournful in spite of her years. Annie Besant lived in this house off and on until the end of the 1910s, but left Europe suddenly for America and India, where she died in Madras on September 20, 1933. By then, the fact that she had been questioned in connection with the Charles Leadbeater scandal had lost any news value.

The Theosophists were still around at the beginning of the '20s, but they were becoming less popular. People increasingly were combining vague ideas about spirituality and religion with an interest in the occult and notions of higher planes of existence and purity. A vague socialism was often added to this mixture, as was vegetarianism and a belief in the beneficial effects of outdoor sports. By the '30s, quasi-mystical nationalistic ideas were merging with the worship of the body beautiful. One outcome of these developments was the branch of populist biology known as "racial biology" in which the perfect human, the *man*, was seen as the evolutionary ideal.

Annie Besant would have recognised none of this.

I put my cigarette out in the grass. Siralee is coming towards me.

We both hear the voices, but cannot see the boys. Siralee has switched off the torch and is looking at me anxiously. The cat, just a swift grey shadow, disappears under a bush. I wish I could hide as easily. The voices are in the garden. They are shouting at each other, barking like two angry dogs.

"Why the fuck dinn't you tell the cunt to fuckin shut 'er face an' let 'er go. Fuckin stopid."

"You shut yer face, you fuckin shit. Look 'ere, who's bleedin? I'm fuckin bleedin. Find me someat to tie round it, for fuck's sake. She won't forget what'a gave 'er. She won't knife nobody no more. No more, ever."

Then come sounds of crashing stones when the first speaker dashes out of the garden through a gap in the wall. He's moving so quickly that he's almost flying, his arms and his open jacket flapping. After a few seconds, the other boy, the bleeding one, leaves the same way, running clumsily, bent over double and swearing, fuck, fuck, fuck, as if it was a health-giving mantra. I catch a glimpse of his shaved head and white face, thin and vulnerable as a child's. Two young boys, but they have knifed somebody. Some cunt who tried to defend herself.

Slowly, I follow them through the gap to see if I can find her in the street, but it is empty.

*

Gupta phones the police while I sit down and light another cigarette. By now, my hands are shaking so much that I give up trying to smoke and crush the fag in an ashtray. Siralee has settled in one of the large armchairs, sinking out of sight. The food smells are still about, but cold, stale and unappetising, like fat congealing in an unwashed pan. The candles have been snuffed, and the feeble ceiling light casts shadows in every nook and cranny.

When the police car arrives half an hour later, we are all still sitting there. We have very little to report. Two young skinheads overheard talking about an assault. One of them is injured. Both might be on drugs.

The uniformed constable is a small, tough and strong-looking man with red hair and pale, buttery skin. He keeps coming back to the question of what *we* were up to in the garden.

What am I working on? How long am I staying in the UK? He avoids looking right at me, instead studying the stained ceiling, presumably because he is shorter than I am.

"We wanted same air," I tell him. "I'm a photographer. I don't know how long I'll be staying." I speak slowly and precisely to give him a chance to get his notes right the first time. I get the feeling that I might well be arrested for Aggravated Listening in Gardens.

Then he starts on Siralee. Is she a British citizen? When was her citizenship confirmed?

Finally, he walks round the garden, afterwards making a note of his effective working time (sixty minutes). He didn't find a woman, but did find a great deal of blood on the ground and on the wall. Before leaving, he tells us that a photographer will be along as soon as it is light enough. He takes down our telephone numbers. If only it could be established that the blood comes from British heterosexuals, his interest in the case might increase.

His car engine roars into life as he steps on the accelerator.

*

Nat, Rea and Siralee clear the table in silence. Rea moves slowly. Her heavy body, wrapped in a yellow housecoat, waddles to and fro. Siralee quickly piles up bowls, plates and glasses and stacks them in the large old-fashioned kitchen sink. Nat supervises the work, picking slowly at breadcrumbs which the careless ladies have dropped on the floor. I'm hiding in the armchair Siralee has just left, and Gupta is sitting on the sofa.

"Dreadful," he keeps saying at regular intervals.

No-one else speaks. The clattering of dishes in the kitchen and the thudding of a large fly against the lampshade seem to deepen the silence in the room, shut off by the darkness outside the windows.

The faithless cat pads in again and curls up at my feet. For once,

I'm glad of its casual companionship. We sit for a long time, while Nat falls asleep and Rea and Siralee start chatting in the kitchen. Finally, Gupta goes to bed, and I wander upstairs.

I cannot help remembering Myrtle Black's recollection of what happened to her more than half a century ago, as vivid as my own memory of what just happened to me. I wonder, yet again, if I would have seen more if only I had been looking through a camera lens, or maybe from far away in time. It's impossible to know.

August 10 and 11, 1905

"WOULD YOU BELIEVE it, it's by James McNeil Whistler," Stead was saying. "I bought it in a second-hand book-shop in Charing Cross. I bet the man had no idea at all." His voice sounded hoarse and, strangely enough, flat and uninterested.

Jacob was visiting the great man in his office for the second time, walking there through the mostly empty streets. It was just after 6.30 a.m. The room seemed exactly the same in the dusty half-light and was as sticky and hot as last time, in spite of the early hour. Both windows were wide open, but there was no breeze to rustle the manu-scripts on the desk or even stir the proofs drying on the windowsill. The mixed smells of newspaper printing filled the air – sweet paper, acrid printer's ink. On the desk, the bottle of Indian ink still had its top off, as if Stead had just filled his pen.

The editor turned to his visitor looking surprised, almost as if he had been caught out. He had been examining a sketch that might have been a study for a bigger painting, but was complete enough to be framed. Stead seemed to think it extraordinarily precious but Jacob, nearly sick with exhaustion, could barely look at it.

It was a view of Wapping Old Stairs with the Thames at low tide. Jacob had walked there more than once, watching the mud grip the moored ships and speculating about the grim old tradition of displaying executed villains in iron cages chained to the steps. The artist had showed barges and elegant sailing-ships leaning this way and that as if in a storm, emphasising the depth and succulence of the river mud with quick little graphite lines. In the foreground, he had drawn the blurred outlines of two ragged children raking the exposed bank with long sticks, looking for metal objects, coins, intact pottery or lumps of coal – anything that could be turned into money or warmth.

Leaning forward to look at the drawing, Jacob came close enough to Stead to register an odd smell. It was the sour odour of fear. The man's eyes were bloodshot with strain, as if Stead too had been up all night. His hair and beard looked unkempt, and greying stubble grew stiffly on his cheeks.

"I watched that boy run away last night. It *was* a boy, not a spirit! You know that too. I want to know what the children are doing there!" Jacob said abruptly, hardly recognising his own hoarse voice, and fell silent again as suddenly.

"What is being done to them?" he asked after a pause, trying to sound calmer. Waiting for Stead to answer, he felt that his tiredness was making him register every detail about the man in front of him as exactly as a photographic plate might.

Stead propped his picture gently on the mantelpiece. Then he sat down heavily on the chair behind his desk and seemed to study his hands, placing them palms down on the desktop. Their appearance suggested the hands of a gentleman despite the faint rims of dirt under the nails.

Because the presses were silent, they could hear mumbling, rattling noises from the editorial office. Now and then the telephone rang with a funny animal sound. Stead broke the silence.

"I must make it clear that I am in *no way* involved. I had no idea of this . . . business. Of Pastor Leadbeater being allowed such liberties. I had simply no idea . . ." His voice trailed off. Then he spoke again.

"Leadbeater is acting in a completely outrageous manner. He's completely mad." Stead looked up at Jacob, his eyes surprisingly quick and appraising. Almost cunning.

Jacob was too tired to attempt to work out what Stead meant.

By now, newspaper boys were crowding into the yard below, ready to collect the new editions. For the rest of the day, they would cry their wares all over town. As Jacob listened to the everyday sounds of talking and laughing in the yard, each voice seemed to grow louder and echo between the walls.

A horse clattered into the yard through the vaulted gateway, pulling a laden carriage with iron-clad wheels across the cobbles. Jacob had a vision of the god Tor driving to war in a chariot drawn by rams.

The editor W. T. Stead gave *Pall Mall Gazette* a liberal, tolerant profile, and it sold steadily, with a print run on the order of 20,000. It included interviews, the style was lively and the content was illustrated with photographs and drawings. Stead became well known as a champion of the weak and in particular for his support of abandoned women and children. At one point, he went to prison for publishing a series of sharply critical articles. For many years, he worked for The Federation, a working party with members drawn from many European countries. Its aim was a joint British and European enactment of laws to criminalise prostitution. Seven years after the events described here, Stead would get first-hand experience of fatalities on a large scale. He and most of the other passengers on the White Star Line's steamship *Titanic* drowned during the night April 14–15, 1912.

Stead slowly pulled the windows shut, his movements as deliberate as a sleepwalker's.

"Please tell me about it. What he's up to?" Jacob urged.

Stead looked at his hands again for a moment and decided that he had to speak.

"Our photographer, Herbert Burrows, was engaged to photograph the proceedings," he began, staring at the desktop. All around the room, there were piles of papers, manuscripts and books stacked on the dark, varnished floor.

"Leadbeater wanted to be able to see for himself, to record the state of their bodies, the colour of their auras, any changes in temperature, movements and . . . certain changes that allegedly appear moments before . . . well, I don't know. I don't think anybody understands this, but before something . . . as he puts it, 'leaves the body'. It's all very complicated. They take a lot of sequential photographs, a series of twelve exposures according to this man Eadweard Muybridge's method. And they change the light levels. I don't grasp the technicalities, well, not exactly. I've never attended those sessions."

Another pause.

Stead poured himself a glass of water from a carafe on the desk, but didn't offer Jacob any. His hand was not steady; glass rattled against glass. The water looked turbid, like pond-water. Stead swallowed some with difficulty, his beard becoming wet round his mouth.

"What do the pictures look like?"

"I've been given to understand that 'something' is visible on a handful of exposures, some kind of indeterminate shapes. But then, the quality generally is not satisfactory, and there are quite a few spots and what not on the negatives. Burrows knows this kind of thing, so he can tell you everything about . . . the technicalities. By the way, Leadbeater says that Burrows is earning a great deal of money for this job."

Stead stopped speaking again. He pulled a small penknife from his waistcoat pocket and absent-mindedly started cleaning his nails, apparently less tense now. He cast another appraising glance at Jacob, in whose eyes he had surely retrieved his position by explaining the scientific background, simply and factually. A straightforward investigative story, that was all. Nothing to do with him personally.

His slim hands were still trembling, however.

"What happens to the photographs?"

"Pastor Leadbeater keeps them."

"What about Mrs Besant?"

"Annie knows nothing about this! Nor did I, until a couple of days ago. Come to think of it, you're involved too."

"And that boy – he did get away, didn't he?"

"It was never anyone's intention that Tom would participate in the
. . . experiments. He was Annie's foster-child, if you like. Of course,
Charles was supposed to be in charge of him when Annie wasn't
there." Stead shook his head as he said this, apparently hardly able
to believe Jacob's ignorance.

"Tom had been helping out, put it that way," Stead went on.
"Fetching water, wiping up spills, carrying coal for the stove. That sort
of thing. He kept the photographic fluids at the right temperature.
Poured the boys' baths. Whatever." He flung his arms wide, almost
overturning the carafe. The surface slopped over the line left at its
former level.

"The boys had to be clean, you see. Any dirt at all on their bodies,
and the results would be less good. Possibly useless. Or so I'm told.
By the way, Pastor Leadbeater does all his own processing now that
Burrows has taught him the ropes."

Stead thought for a moment.

"I'm sure Tom will be back. After all, there's nowhere for him to
go. Nobody would believe him or even listen to what he's got to say.
A little Irish vagabond from an orphanage. Though it must be said
the lad's remarkably smart. He can even read and write."

"He's got a father who wants to look after him. The father turned
up yesterday and didn't like what he saw. Isn't that right?"

"We – Annie and I – have already spoken to the man about his
son's disappearance, and he seems to understand the situation.
Naturally, we'll do our best to find Tom." Stead leaned forward over
the desk, and once more Jacob sensed his fear.

"We're trying to avoid negative publicity, do you understand? This
mustn't come out the wrong way. Surely you can sympathise with that
idea? Leadbeater has been stopped and the rest of the children taken
into proper care. Well, they've been sent back."

Jacob did not say anything, only observed Stead as he turned back
to the windows. Did he want to keep an eye on who came and went
across the yard?

"How many children?" Jacob finally asked.

"Five," Stead replied, after thinking for a moment. Then he opened the window. The racket in the yard had finished, but still no air entered the room.

*

Jane Addercot said nothing, on purpose, when she unlocked the three locks on the door to let Jacob in at 7, Sussex Gardens. She stepped aside, and he passed her quickly, saying nothing except "Good morning, Miss."

He took the narrow staircase in a few long strides, aware that a powerful trail of odours was following him, thankfully dominated by Pear's lavender soap. It was just past 9 a.m. The landlady remained at the bottom of the stairs, staring curiously and rather disapprovingly at his disappearing back.

Miss Addercot had been running her highly respectable boarding house in Paddington for twenty years. She intended to have a word with young Mr Hall that afternoon. Tomorrow, Mr Hall must move out, vacating his room by noon. She closed the door firmly behind her when she returned to her own rooms. Not that she was of a nervous disposition, she told herself, but one could never be too careful. He had smelled as if he had spent the night in some kind of vagrants' hostel. Mr Hall may well have had an English-sounding name, but a foreigner he was, no question about it.

She returned to her cup of tea and the morning paper. Miss Addercot took the *Daily Mail*, and that morning it had a most interesting article about German spies. She pressed her thin lips together. Perhaps she should clean that room as soon as possible. Better get another paying guest in promptly.

*

Jacob's room had a window to the street, level with the row of large trees along the pavement. Their branches were so close that they knocked against his windowpanes and kept his room in a constant dank shade. A faint smell of mould hovered about the furnishings, and leaving the window open had its own drawbacks in the form of dust and insects. He would never forget an army of small beetles marching in long lines along the windowsill as if hypnotised by its off-white surface. Later, he found many dead specimens on the floor and was able to examine their yellow and black carapaces.

With an effort, he pulled off his clothes, crawled under the blanket and felt tiredness break over him like a great wave. He fell asleep.

He woke as suddenly. He had been dreaming about ropes, big untidy balls of them pushed into a tin chest. He knew he had seen a chest just like that recently, but could not bring the memory into full consciousness. It was getting dark, and his watch told him that it was almost 8 p.m.

The smell of boiled gammon and cabbage drifted through from the kitchen, and even though it wasn't very appealing, it made him realise how hungry he was. It wasn't likely that he could persuade Miss Addercot to heat some supper for him. He lit the gaslight flame and shuffled over to the commode to drink some water from the jug, almost emptying it. The water was stale, but it filled his stomach and made the hunger-pangs less noticeable for a while.

With the rest of the water, he washed his face and his thin chest and arms. Putting on clean clothes, he looked at his face in the mirror. It was as if a stranger was looking back at him, although definitely someone he had seen before. His features – the strong nose, the slightly weak mouth, the grey eyes – were the same. He put some water on his comb and slicked back his rather long hair before putting on a clean collar.

It was surprisingly easy to pack his things, although his hands had been ill used during his clambering over the wall. Jacob travelled light. All he owned could easily be carried. His camera, of course, and his suitcase for clothes. He had bought a few books and pictures, mostly Japanese prints. Jacob felt positively glad to be leaving the room and Miss Addercot, and for a while the relief filled his thoughts.

Then he realised that he had been thinking about the little girl – Dora, her name was – in spite of not having seen her since the day in July when he had first met Annie Besant. He wondered if Dora was also one of Leadbeater's "protégés". Then he thought that Stead had been right and that he, Jacob, was involved in whatever was going on in his capacity as Herbert Burrows's assistant. Then the memory of the dog came back to him, and especially its odd, almost unreal disappearance down the empty street.

He sat down on the edge of the bed and pulled the dead man's wallet from the pocket of his own filthy jacket.

*

The wallet did not contain any money. There was a postcard from New York, still damp from water – or maybe blood. He put it carefully to the side and studied a seaman's letter of accreditation, registered in the name of Michael Flaherty. There was a receipt for wages paid – all of £20. Jacob thought this a really large sum. Where had it gone? Then he found Annie Besant's visiting card.

Next to the letter of accredition and partly hidden by it was a list of names and addresses. Or was it? The names were unreal, theatrical, more than a little absurd: Count of Ortranto, Jago, Caliban. The addresses were as unlikely, mostly large public places: Piccadilly Circus, Charing Cross, Fleet Street. Only one name seemed familiar: Gatti's Music Hall. There were no numbers, no dates or times of day. The handwriting was a little uneven, the letters apparently having been printed with deliberation and some effort. The pen had been held so firmly at times that the nib had gone through the paper.

Jacob read through the list again before putting it in his pocket together with the postcard. Then he closed Flaherty's big leather wallet and hid it at the bottom of his suitcase. Miss Addercot seemed amazingly friendly when he met her, standing in the doorway to her cosy sitting room. The smell of cooking was overwhelming, but not enough to hide the stout on Miss Addercot's breath.

She told him that Annie Besant had called to enquire about his plans, but that they had decided not to disturb him as he was asleep.

"Very nice. Such a lady," Miss Addercot said with her rarely practised smile. "So refined." She was almost curtseying where she stood, but her stiff knees couldn't quite manage it, and instead she wobbled a little.

Miss Addercot regretted that Jacob could not stay on, she said, but she understood how it was with young men.

"You'd like to see the sights, move around the city – perfectly understandable! Though I shall have to ask for one day's extra rent, seeing that you've given me such short notice."

*

It was only when Jacob was standing in the street, watching the carriages rattle past, that it dawned on him that he had no plans at all – well, except for going to see Albert at Drury Lane. He could ask Albert for advice and maybe also to be allowed to kip on his floor for a bit. So far, Albert was his only real friend in the huge city. Still, he would have to tell his story to Herbert Burrows, if only the man were sober enough to get the general drift.

Then suddenly the memory came back to him – the chest with the ropes that he had seen so clearly in his dream was real all right. He now knew where he had seen it. It was in Herbert Burrows's dusty backyard. Burrows had not been keeping ropes in the chest, but images painted on canvas. Pictures of endless seas, gentle woodland, painted studio backdrops well on their way to terminal decay, covered with rot and spots of mould, with fungi growing on pale blue skies and dry cracks running across yellow junks and sampans off the docks in Yokohama or Shanghai. The Far Eastern ones had been used as backgrounds for portraits of tough tea-clipper captains.

They were the remains of Herbert Burrows's time as an established photographer, his time of real success. The kids used to like rooting around in the chest, and in the end Burrows had padlocked it.

*

On Friday, August 11, the sun disappeared in an ochre-coloured haze. It was still very warm, but the oppressive, electrifying threat of a thunderstorm hovered in the hot air. The dry grass was full of insects Jacob had never seen before, dragonflies and shimmering beetles resembling tropical species. Even the grasshoppers seemed larger than usual, and the parkland resounded with their grinding song.

Jacob had been strolling on Hampstead Heath for most of the day. It was just about as far as possible from the house in Lansdowne Road. In the morning, he had scanned all the newspapers he could lay his hands on, but there were no reports of anyone finding a corpse. Either they had not discovered Flaherty's body, or maybe someone had moved it.

Jacob had spent the night in the simple house in Hampstead that Albert shared with some friends. It was in a quiet cul-de-sac, a quite rural place on the edge of the great park. A rough grassy slope opened up behind the outhouses. The house had been a smithy once, and the low, dark rooms with their thick walls and heavily plastered chimney-pieces seemed to Jacob still to smell of iron and heat.

He liked wandering over the Heath, which was more like wild wood-land than a park. The hot summer had left its mark in dried-up streams in deep ravines and a number of dead trees. Blackbirds and starlings were everywhere, picking vigorously among the dead leaves, sorting and passing or rejecting their finds – true little bureaucrats in the tall counting-chambers of the woods. Now and then, one of the birds stopped to listen, its eyes like bright buttons, but the large wooded area was almost empty of humans on this hot afternoon.

The long drought had intensified and concentrated the scents of the sweet-smelling canopies of leaves and the still damp soil near the root systems of the ancient oaks. Jacob pushed through the vegeta-tion almost hiding a winding path. Huge stands of lovage filled the air with their spicy smell of liquorice. Hairy seed capsules, tough small containers of life, stuck to his clothes. Now and then, he sat on the grass, enjoying the warmth of the sun-baked soil coming through his clothes.

He had been pondering what to do all day. In the still park, last night seemed unreal. After all, he had no proof of anything. Tom had disappeared. The people attending yesterday's seance were unlikely to admit to having been there, let alone state that they had seen a spiritual manifestation running around the room. As for Michael Flaherty, only Annie Besant, Stead, maybe Burrows and himself knew the man's identity. Well, and Pastor Leadbeater, but he wasn't going to be much help.

The only thing seemed to be to wait for the body to be found and for the police to start investigating. For a moment, Jacob regretted removing the wallet, but, on the other hand, the murderer – or murderers – would almost certainly have done the same later on. He or they might of course have stolen the money and left the rest. The London police would be satisfied only when they knew the dead man's identity. Flaherty was just another beaten-up and knifed sailor who had been robbed, but an anonymous victim meant that the investigation could not be closed.

Jacob had an idea of where the papers he had found might lead him. He pulled out the list of fantasy names again.

Suppose the names were pseudonyms for customers and maybe deliveries, he thought. The goods were Leadbeater's pictures. If so, the times and dates might be fixed and so had not been worth noting down. Or maybe that side of things was unknown to whoever had given Flaherty the information.

Jacob picked up a stone heated by the sun from the dry bed of a small stream that at another time would have been dancing along at the bottom of the slope. When he wiped the dried yellow mud from it, he found that it was a smooth blue flint that rested easily in his hand.

Next, he thought, suppose that Flaherty visited some of these places during the last evening he was alive. Maybe someone – could it have been Annie Besant? – gave him enough information to carry on looking for his son. But why? The boy was still in the house. Or was he?

Jacob got up and walked up one of the green hills with a wide view of London, the Thames an undulating band of hammered silver on the horizon. The blue of the sky had deepened, and in the far distance it was almost black. Roofs and spires glowed in the slanting rays of sunlight with a new, even richer radiance, as if made of mercury or gold-veined ore. The air became tinged with a faint smell of sulphur as the clouds drew closer together with dull rumbling sounds. Then a flash of lightning swept across the sky, the thunder following it immediately. The straggling cluster of trees on top of Queen Boadicea's ancient tumulus was rustling in the hot wind. The slender trees looked as if they were searching for support, frightened of losing their grip.

Jacob closed his eyes. He tried to conjure up an image of the little boy – scared, pale, tired, his hair wet with sweat and . . . spattered with mud. Now the answer seemed obvious. The boy had come in from outside. He had not emerged from Leadbeater's experimental eyrie in the attic. He was returning to the place he knew, because, like Jacob himself, he had nowhere else to go.

The heavy drops were falling like hammer blows, creating little craters in the dry soil. All Jacob could do was run for the protective woods before the whole Heath disappeared behind a steaming grey wall of rain.

The Photographer, I

JACOB KNOCKED AGAIN, harder than before. The knocks echoed in the narrow road, and a man shouted at him from a window to stop making so much noise. It was almost 8 p.m. – supper time in the many small homes. The air was heavy with the smells of hot lard and frying bread. Jacob could hear Burrows pottering around inside his studio. The photographer seemed to be talking to himself, a long conversation with complicated questions and answers.

It had been raining all afternoon, but now it had cleared a little. Heavy clouds were piling up around the hills above London, making the city the eye of the storm, where it was still calm.

Jacob decided to walk round to the back, following the narrow lane that ran along one side of the studio. Puddles had formed in potholes among the dirty cobbles, and the smell from heaps of old garbage was almost unbearable, especially around a dead rat lying by the wall, its belly swollen and its legs pointing straight into the air. Jacob cautiously made his way through the mess, holding his folded handkerchief in front of his nose and mouth. When he happened to nudge the brick wall, it felt soft, like moss or thick cloth. The studio had a window facing the lane, and through it he could dimly see Burrows inside. The photographer had lit three candles in a candlestick on a bench by the window, and there was no other source of light. He was sitting on the floor, sorting through things in boxes. Jacob knocked on the window, and Burrows looked up, obviously frightened. Then he recognised Jacob, relaxed and signed that he would come to the back door.

When he opened the door, Herbert Burrows looked confused, as if he had only just woken up. This impression was strengthened by the fact that he was wearing a long, creased shirt dangling loose round his thin legs. The yard was empty. Jacob glanced quickly at the corner with the old chest containing the backdrops, feeling relieved for some reason. Burrows carefully locked and bolted the door behind them.

It looked as if Burrows was preparing to move. There were lots of rough wooden boxes, and bottles of chemicals stood about on the floor. His old black trousers were hanging up to dry in front of the stove, where the fire had gone out. The room was unaired and damp.

Burrows went to light some more candles before bending over one of the boxes to look for something. After searching for a while, he produced a photograph. It was an old studio portrait mounted on stiff grey vellum.

"Look, this is Beth and me, just after our engagement. It was a lovely sunny day in April, and we had gone for an excursion to Richmond. The year was 1868. A friend took the picture; he had a studio down by the river. It was a grand day."

He held out the photo and waved Jacob closer. Jacob leaned into the circle of light, staring at the picture. Was Herbert Burrows the slim young man who held himself so straight, looking directly ahead with confident eyes? His black moustache had been waxed; his best suit fitted him well and looked neatly brushed. The girl at his side seemed fragile and pale in her high-necked white dress. She was leaning on Burrows, her slim hand resting on his arm. The backdrop was a bright but decorous landscape, a park with geometrically aligned woods and a little temple or folly sketched in on top of a hill in the far distance.

"I've come to ask you about the Flahertys. Do you know what's going on, what happened last night?" Jacob asked uncertainly, still holding the photograph.

Herbert did not seem to have heard the question.

"My Beth died a couple of days ago," he said, taking his photo back quickly. "Nothing else matters now."

He shuffled across the room to his workbench, barefoot and trembling but intent on getting another lot of brown bottles down from the shelves. He must have cut himself earlier, because there were brown stains here and there on the floor.

Then he turned abruptly.

"Both Flahertys are dead now, aren't they?" he almost shouted. "Father and son. The poor little lad looked as dead as a doornail, blue in the face and gone really stiff. But that was down by the river, and there's no telling how he got back into the house again. I don't know. Ask His Bloody Reverend Satan himself! You know where to find him. At Lansdowne Road, upstairs in that flaming attic!"

He hauled another packed box across the floor, found an empty one and filled it quickly. He was working at a frantic pace unlike anything Jacob had seen him equal before. His face had become reddened and shiny, his hair was hanging down in sweaty strands, and his shirt stuck damply to his back and chest.

The studio was filling with the familiar piercing smell of chemicals, but it had a sulphurous overtone, suggesting that something dangerous had leaked from a cracked receptacle. It was becoming hard to breathe. The candles and Burrows's movements made sudden shadows flit across the white-limed walls.

The room resembled a cave, with the emptying shelves and cupboards opening like crevices and passages leading deeper inwards.

*

After a while, Burrows stopped working as suddenly as if a spring had broken inside him.

"I liked both the women, you know," he said. "The old Russian one was grand, I mean that Blavatsky lady. She knew her job all right, every trick in the book. When she was in charge, it was all go – knocking and voices and lights and so on – and she could predict the future at the drop of a hat. Great ability, she had. It helped that she could drink anybody under the table if she had to. Now, Annie Besant is different. She's a much more serious person. I don't think she ever suspected Helena Blavatsky of deception. There was a lot of talk, naturally, what with the two women, a mysterious Russian and a divorced Irishwoman, living alone together in a big house. Rumours of all kinds of improper goings-on. No question about it. Witches, tribades, all sorts. Nothing I could be bothered with."

Burrows fell silent again, peering short-sightedly at the label on a rusty old tin. It started to rain, and the wind drove large drops against the windows, making a sound as if someone was throwing fistfuls of gravel at them.

"I was interested in chemistry when I was young . . ." Burrows muttered. "You know, the composition of matter. The behaviour of substances. This here tin, it contains a sulphurous compound." He put the tin down again with a trembling hand.

"Tell me, what happened to Mick Flaherty?"

"He followed me from Lansdowne Road. I didn't notice him, so he must have been very quiet. I walked round to Gatti's because I know one of the serving girls, and . . . well, I felt lonely. He turned up there. A right odd character, if you ask me."

"I do. How do you mean, 'odd'?"

"Take his manner. He was dressed like a common sailor, but he was well spoken – almost like a gentleman. I got the idea he was acting a role in a play. At the same time, there was something weird about the way he ogled me. Something . . . inhuman. I can't explain why, but he made me uneasy. He had a funny smell about him too. A strong smell. Anyway, he started questioning me. Wanted to know about Besant and the boys. I don't know how he had found out about the boys. And he wanted to know about Charles Leadbeater. Right enough, I had no intention of protecting that bastard. I don't need his money. Not any more." Burrows found a dirty cloth, blew his nose and wiped his mouth hard.

"He kept at it, asking questions, being ingratiating, offering me more beer and so on. I told him what I knew, and that was a good feeling, I can tell you. I described the photographic business and the trade and all the rest. I never earned much from it, you know. Just enough to pay for Beth, that's all. Most of the pictures were harmless little dressing-up jobs that financed Leadbeater's so called 'real research'. He knew lots of go-betweens; they handled the sales. I don't know anything about the business side."

*

The storm had moved in a wide circle, first to the coast and then, driven away by the sea, in over the hot inland counties. Now it was back, rumbling directly above Burrows's studio. Gusts of wind drove the heavy rain, turning the backyard into a mud-pit. Jacob wondered if the old tin chest would sink with its contents or if it was sealed tightly enough to float. The room's warped ceiling creaked under the weight of the water. Burrows looked up anxiously.

"Where did you find the children?"

"Leadbeater brought them. Ships' lads who'd run away, foundlings from orphanages, you name it – London is full of them. They were grateful to be in a place where they were given a roof over their heads, food and some clothes. Pastor Leadbeater is highly regarded by the poor-law boards, and knowing people like Mrs Besant and Mr Stead meant that it wasn't thought politic to question him."

"What about Tom?"

"Annie Besant was his guardian. But Tom was clever, very bright indeed, and because of that his reactions were especially interesting. He could express himself, could Tom. He might tell us what he experienced. The rule was that Tom mustn't be put at risk, but that didn't stop Leadbeater. He had to test some new stimulating concoction. Afterwards, everything went straight to Hell with no stops on the way. You see, at first we used tincture of opium, but only some of the children ever hallucinated. The rest were completely knocked out and too drowsy to do anything at all. Leadbeater was after a purer drug, strong but without all these side effects. He had heard of this plant the American Indians used and had chased up a cache of dried leaves during one of his travels. He gave the lot to me to play around with. I prepared a highly concentrated extract. Leadbeater tried a very small dose – about 2 milligrams – on four

–161–

boys straight away. Tom got the same dose a bit later on. We got sensational results, and Leadbeater reckoned that the potion was harmless, maybe even good for you, because the boys seemed just fine at first. Then the attacks started, after about twenty-four hours. Spasms, they were, repeating again and again. The more they came back, the more frightening it was. The drug had a runaway effect, you see. We didn't give the boys any more of the drug. It was so strong, it seemed they were burning up inside."

"What about the rope?"

"It had nothing to do with them dying! And you must believe this, the boys were very willing to participate. They didn't mind testing the drug, and they trusted the pastor, of course. I fancy they thought the whole thing quite exciting. After all, it was their chance to experience things no-one they knew had ever even dreamed of."

"What happened to Flaherty?"

"I never saw him again. Beer makes me sleepy. You know that. I was sitting there, nodding a bit, and when I came to, he was gone. Like a flaming spy!"

"Where did you take them? I mean, what did you do with the boys' bodies?"

"Leadbeater knew a place by the river, behind Victoria Station. They're bringing a new line in and have been digging all summer. No-one would think anything of disturbed ground round there. Besides, the mud seems bottomless."

They had to walk in the pouring rain all the way to St Paul's before they found a free hire carriage. Burrows kept muttering and trying to turn back, but Jacob held on to the photographer's arm. A stream was flowing down Ludgate Hill and rushing into the drains at the bottom. Once in the carriage, they looked through the rain-streaked windows at passers-by hurrying about in the downpour like ghosts.

Fleet Street looked as if the medieval river beneath it had returned to the surface, and by the time they reached the Trafalgar Square end of the Strand, the coachman said he wanted to stop, refusing to take his passengers any further, at least not without a better fare. Having no more money to offer him, they had to get out.

The huge square was empty, and all around them the storm roared and crashed like iron shields banging in ancient battles. The lightning cut jagged, flaring slashes in the solid grey of the sky.

Jacob grabbed Burrows's arm to propel him to the Underground station, but the man resisted like a hooked fish, his mouth half open and his whole being rigid with negativity.

They caught a train to Victoria in the end, but getting around outside the station precinct was almost impossible. The whole site was a jumble of ripped-up rails, ropes and pulleys and water-filled ditches. Along Buckingham Palace Road, entire centuries-old blocks of buildings had been demolished to make room for the new tracks and station extension. The gap being dug resembled a ravine. Progress was clearly slow, the work of digging and drilling being uncommonly hard. There were obstacles everywhere below street level, dangerous strata of treacherous quicksand, water-soaked marshes and old bogs stretching down into the original clay of the riverbed. The engineers had designed new layers of varying densities to provide a safe base for the railway running down towards the Thames. Jacob, who had passed the area before in better weather, remembered seeing workmen driving steadying poles into the mud with sledgehammers.

The storm meant that the whole site had been abandoned. Water levels were rising quickly everywhere. White-painted marker posts, some with crossbars to show the correct height of draining ditches, leaned in all directions, looking in the deepening gloom like plain crosses in a dismal cemetery. A heavy odour of rot hung over the scarred land caused by oxygen reaching long-buried roots and marshland plants.

Burrows led the way, climbing a low, tarred fence supported by upright sleepers like gateposts to an unknown world. The photographer seemed to have reconciled himself to being the guide. He moved cautiously and kept a close lookout for guards, though not a soul was in sight. He clearly was finding landmarks hard to locate as he struggled through the streaming rain, the sucking mud gripping his feet at every step.

Finally, he stopped next to a long ditch running close to the river-bank. The Thames was flowing fast now, carrying huge volumes of water that, before the embankments were built, would have flooded low-lying reaches of London and turned the land back to what it once had been – marshes steaming in the sun, part of a huge delta. Now the river stayed in its bed, held in check by the long walls along its banks.

Burrows's face was red with effort, and water was streaming off his long black coat. Both he and Jacob were weighed down like deep-water divers by the leaden masses of clay on their boots.

"This is it," Burrows shouted, waving Jacob closer.

They stood side by side staring at the brimming trench in front of them.

"Did you carry them all the way here?"

"Yes, it was night-time and easier going than now. The drought meant that we could take a horse and cart almost all the way. We carried them the last bit, of course. No guards then either." He looked around nervously, but there was no sound except for the monotonous drumming of the rain.

"They had started filling the trench up. The storm must have stopped them from completing the job."

He probed the depth with a pulled-up marker post, looking more like a fisherman now than a fish, practised and motivated.

"Just about 3 feet left, I fancy. The poor lads are buried in a water-filled coffin by now. Well, it was a tin trunk with holes drilled in it, and it sank 8 feet or so. Tom went the same way. His heart had stopped, and he showed no signs of life at all. I held a lit match right in front of his lips myself, and there was not a flicker. He was dead, right enough. The actual chest we jammed in next to the poles. It was hard work, but that bastard Leadbeater is as strong as an ox, I'll say that for him. We had brought spades and forks and what-have-you, but it still took us the best part of an hour to get the hole big enough." He paused, a thought having struck him.

"The chest with the bodies was heavy, of course, so it might well have sunk deeper. Maybe they've already got the cement layer in place on top of it." Burrows crouched and rammed his post down, as if playing with a wooden sword.

They both heard it strike the hard layer below.

"There you are, the cement set quickly in the heat," Burrows said. "That layer is held in place by the poles. It would be just about impossible to get through to the bottom of the trench again."

Jacob probed the muddy water too. A few feet under the surface, the end of the post hit a rough surface. Once the water had drained away, the trench would be filled with sand.

Burrows moved close to him, putting his arm round the boy's shoulders before Jacob had a chance to draw back. He lost his balance for a moment and was close to slipping into the ditch, but Burrows held on to him. The man seemed stronger now. Maybe he had recovered, comforted by the thought that the children's corpses were truly out of the way.

He spoke right into Jacob's ear to make sure he was heard through the roaring of the storm. His breath was warm and human.

"Jacob, you'll want to know this. The boys got a proper funeral. Pastor Leadbeater read the service and everything went according to the rules."

Jacob, speechless, could do nothing but free himself from Burrows's grip.

*

They had no reason to stay. Stumbling back through the building site, they heard a dog barking. The sound seemed to be moving, sometimes right in front of them, sometimes further away. Burrows was swearing and moving quite quickly. Maybe he was afraid of dogs or of guards – or of guard-dogs. Finally, the barking died away.

Jacob's eyes had got used to the dark, but he still found it hard to see where they were going. The slippery path led straight into slimy puddles, forcing them to leave it and take a more round-about route.

The constant changes of direction were unnerving. The site began to look impossibly enormous. Burrows had refused to bring a light, and there was no street lighting left on the site's perimeter. The rain was turning to drizzle, but the sky remained overcast without stars or moon.

Burrows was walking ahead of Jacob when they reached an area where workmen had been just hours earlier and boards had been thrown across ditches to form swaying bridges. Grey drainage pipes criss-crossed the ground like the network of veins in a body.

Burrows stumbled and fell head first into the black water before Jacob knew what was happening. The man did not even cry out, or maybe he decided not to. He sunk like a stone, having fallen into a steep-sided hole with an unfinished row of poles. It seemed bottomless when Jacob probed it with a post. He crawled around for a long time on hands and knees, his hands going white and stiff as he plunged the long post again and again into the depths. Not a single air-bubble rose to the surface.

The photographer Herbert Burrows, in his long overcoat heavy with water, had disappeared.

*

The drizzle was fading, and the water was draining away slowly. The river rats were returning in a sniffing, exploring horde of black and brown bodies, having found refuge from the rising water levels in piles of wooden posts or under workmen's huts. Now they found Jacob and looked at him with tiny, bright eyes. One of them, a very large, shiny male, seemed to be their leader as well as a heavyweight fighter, judging by the bite across his back. Padding ahead of the rest, he slipped into the water, swimming in wide circles. His pale feet moved swiftly, like little propellers.

The Photographer, II

IT DOESN'T EVEN look like blood. I don't know what I expected, but not this lot of messy brown stains, barely visible here and there among the fallen bricks.

The police photographer rang the doorbell insistently just after 8 a.m. Amazingly, the apparatus decided to respond with a trembling noise like a disused voice. The Gupta household showed no sign of life, so I decided to answer the door.

Before running downstairs, I pull on jeans and a T-shirt. I can't find a comb. Never mind; this guy is a police photographer and has seen worse things. After a certain amount of pushing and pulling, I get the front door open. Still, it isn't that hard, and I ask myself why Gupta never uses this entrance.

The man at the door is middle-aged, short and a little overweight. Jacob would probably have called him plump in a sneering voice. It's the kind of pale, bluish fat that you put on when you spend hours hanging out in cars, waiting. His skin is tensed over the tissues underneath, like a slug's; it looks like it's about to burst open. This effect is enhanced by a silky, shiny black pilot's jacket.

He shows me a greasy police ID. His name is Al Something. Al and I walk together into the garden to have a look at the crime scene. We have to make our way through Gupta's hall and sitting room. He has left his front door unlocked, but closed the bedroom door. Al checks the place out as we walk through, but says nothing.

And no, it doesn't even look like blood. The other bloke hasn't left any tracks, of course. It's hard to feel much at all.

"Have the police found the victim, the woman they attacked?"

Al only shakes his head while he carries on taking pictures, working easily and lighting a new fag with the end of his last one. He's got a neat little Rolleiflex camera and manages to get a lot of close-up hand-print shots. All the while, he's whistling an old Rolling Stones tune, "Ruby Tuesday". I don't want to be impressed by his versatility, but can't help myself. I always fail completely when I try to do more than one thing at a time. Like talking while I'm driving. Or thinking one thing, but saying another.

"Hey, he lost a lot of blood, right? And, hey, five perfectly good fingers and a palm-print, too. They don't come much better than this."

Al doesn't wait for me to answer, just moves around with unexpected agility. The camera shutter hums gently. Straight on, no rubbish. Still "Ruby Tuesday". I wonder if he's got one tune for each day of the week, including Good Friday and Bloody Sunday.

"Still, nothing ever comes from stuff like this. Someone reports trouble, so we do the job. One bloke knifes another bloke. Hell, who cares? They're all the same, these sad bastards. The up side is that they keep their own numbers down. They come out of Notting Hill basements to try a little breaking and entering. And fight each other. I don't think these guys will have a record. Black families, they breed like frigging rats. Just the way they're made, the women drop their babies easy. Though this lot was white, is that right?"

"Very white," I reply, wondering if racism is a basic qualification for joining the force. Al looks pleased with himself. Grinding his fag-end into the path, he restlessly fingers the packet for another one. His face falls like a disappointed child's when it turns out to be empty.

"Anyway. They get into one of these big jobs, sitting here waiting for people with enough cash to renovate them. The developers are on the march actually. Look at Holland Park, all these guys are loaded, I suppose they do writing or creative stuff like that."

Al gives me a critical but brief once-over. He has nothing left to smoke and can't wait to get away. I follow him to his car like the perfect hostess, listen to the engine – "a souped-up Ford 89" – as it roars into action, accompanied by a blast of Mick Jagger in "Honky-Tonk Woman". Al waves to me with his fat little hand, and then he's gone.

The morning is quite lovely, the warm sun making *The Spirit of Nature* seem a bit more cheerful. At least she hasn't fallen over, and the light is turning her veil a pretty pale green. The façade of the house looks more handsome now, with the sunlight reflected in the old French windows. I can see Gupta moving around inside – well, it must be him although I can't be sure.

Annie Besant's rose borders have also emerged from the gloom, and their thick, thorny branches seem set to resist oblivion. Alongside the borders runs what was once a well-constructed sandy path. Islands of white sand, as if from the seaside, still show between invading tufts of grass. I turn round to take in the whole garden, remembering all the people who walked there, talking to each other, thinking . . . living. So many – Yeats, Maud Gonne, the Pankhurst ladies, Shaw, Wells, Leadbeater. And Helena Blavatsky, old, ill and almost immobile.

A deep sigh makes me turn swiftly round.

*

Gupta looks dreadful, grey under his brown skin. There are dark rings under his eyes.

"Has he left?" Gupta's voice is a whine, and he avoids looking at the hole in the garden wall.

"Yes, a few minutes ago. He took pictures of the handprint, but said it probably can't be identified," I tell him, wondering what it is about Gupta that always makes me feel so coarse and brutal. It's *his* fucking responsibility, after all – *his* garden, *his* house.

He seems relieved to hear that the photographer has been, anyway. The usually very neat Gupta has dressed carelessly this morning. The rolls of fluffy red sweater round his stomach make him look like a dishevelled Father Christmas somehow confused about the time of year – or maybe he's more like one of these gnomes living underground who can move about in earth and rock as easily as through air. Gupta has this magic ability to materialise soundlessly.

The door to the garden is not properly closed, and the cat sneaks out, advancing in stops and starts through the long grass. Her tail sweeps from side to side, and she walks almost on tiptoe, presumably because she doesn't like the dew and the damp, soft mosses underfoot. She's like a tiny tiger in a miniature jungle.

"Your friend called," Gupta says, pulling himself together enough to produce a bleak smile. "Miss Darken? She sounded very anxious to speak to you."

"I'll ring her back," I reply, but Gupta seems unwilling to let the subject go. Or maybe it's my company he clings to. I note that he's also wearing a pair of baggy trousers in an implausibly checked material. This must be his cosy at-home outfit rather than whatever he wears for consultations. So, today P. V. Gupta is taking the day off work. He must be worried.

"Is Miss Darken interested in the events that took place round Mrs Besant and the Theosophical movement?"

"Not especially, but I've asked her to help me with a few things."
Gupta peers at me. His face looks a little more normal.

"As a matter of fact, I've been thinking. I believe I might have some information about Annie Besant's last days here. Alas, during that time, she truly found that a medium's powers can be a heavy burden."

"How do you mean?"

"There are certain notes, not yet published – not at all for public consumption. Concerning the occult. Yes, and many are of a very private nature. You could say that the Theosophical movement has not yet considered the time suitable. These notes have been kept here, rather than in the open archive. That's mainly why I'm here. As the guardian – the curator of documents." Gupta's voice trails off, and he looks modestly at his slippers. Evidently, he enjoys his secret knowledge.

"So you've read these notes?"

"Selected items, yes."

"And . . . ?"

"Some passages from the years around 1905 – well, they concern the young girl. Dora. And her disappearance. Mrs Besant also kept notes of events at the time of a police investigation. Word for word. And she described a man who'd broken into the house. And quotes from the questioning afterwards." Gupta sighs as if all this reminds him of yesterday's painful business.

"Would you let me read the notes?"

Gupta hesitates. His secret makes him important, but at the same time he must be able to provide me with enough information to maintain his status. It is like a mental market-stall. The goods are on display; lengths of fine material are pulled out from the rolls. Now is the time to bargain about the price.

"Now, should the police require . . ." Gupta stops, looks nervously about, but the only other living being present is the podgy cat, now lazily stretched out in the sun with its eyes half-open. Gupta pulls himself together.

"Should the police wonder about my role here, as the guardian, if you like, it must be said that it's not strictly official. More like a kind of . . . agreement . . ." Gupta stops again.

"I won't say anything, unless they ask me directly, of course." Actually, I don't think the police will do anything of the sort. Besides, I've no idea what's going on, but I like Gupta and don't care if he's here on some scam.

"I'll say that, as far as I know, Mr Gupta is employed as a consultant and curator. And that's that." I can see that he's not entirely satisfied with my answer, but that's as much as I can promise him. I turn and walk towards the house.

Gupta flutters after me. It seems that he has got something more to tell me.

But I don't think so, not yet. For the moment, all I want to know are the *precise facts* – times, dates, places.

"Where are the documents?"

"In Mrs Besant's old study. Off the landing. And there are some photographs as well. Maybe your friend would be interested to see them?"

"That's quite likely," I tell him.

The Notes

GUPTA FUSSES AHEAD to show me to Annie Besant's study, a room I have not yet seen. Reginald Mortimer set out on a trip abroad just after completing the design of the house, leaving the workmen to interpret his drawings as best they could. This is presumably the reason for all the structural oddities in number 17. Besant's study is one of the typical surprises, a hexagonal chamber with three windows facing the garden. During her last years, Mme Blavatsky was installed in the room immediately below the study as she was unable to climb the stairs. The long-chimneyed stove that used to heat both rooms has of course gone.

Gupta talks on erratically. He mentions that Annie decided to have her study above Madame's bedroom because the Russian lady spent such a lot of her time there. Up to the time of her death in 1891, she would stay in bed all day, receiving visitors propped up on pillows. She communicated with Annie by knocking on the chimney with her stick.

Like the attic, the study has been filled with all kinds of junk, but Annie's desk is still there, screwed to the floor. It's a heavy piece of furniture covered with a dark veneer and has rows of drawers, each with a yellowing ivory knob. Some of the knobs are cracked, making it tricky to pull the drawers out. On the desktop, a muscular bronze tiger stands guard over inkpot and pens. The notes are kept in the bottom drawer, the only one that is locked. Gupta produces a key, and the mechanism responds with a dry little click. The fragile, loose sheets of paper are protected by dark red, marbled cardboard covers held together by pieces of string.

Gently, I open to the first page.

13th August, 1905. Once again, no sleep tonight. The knocking had already begun by midnight and went on, at regular intervals, throughout the night. I cannot think what she really wants from me.

Yesterday, I went through Helena's papers once more, still astonished at how much she knew and, indeed, how much of it has already come true. I found some photographs I had not seen, including to my surprise an image Helena claimed to have been part of a dream. It was a quite small portrait of her taken on the steam ferry from Calais, carelessly developed and discoloured at the rough edges. A few Russian words were scribbled on the back. Could it be a name? I cannot read it. As usual, Helena had been looking straight into the camera, and when I study her image, I feel her presence more strongly then ever before. So many memories have surfaced since, and I have wondered why she was calling them dreams. It could be that she simply did not remember.

Apart from the picture from the ferry, the little collection included photos taken by Herbert Burrows in the garden. We sat for him so very long ago, and it feels strange to sit here now, seeing the same table and chairs outside. The grass needs cutting, but there is no-one here who can do these things any more. People will talk, and it frightens the servants away. I sat at the window for more than an hour yesterday, but could not bring myself to go outside. Charles's cat has found a comfortable place in one of the chairs. I must do something about her. She's getting old and smelly.

30th August, 1905. The police have been here. At first, I thought they might have found one of the children, but they turned out to have come on another errand. A quite young man was questioning me. His suit was ill fitting and his shirt-collar too wide for his thin neck. Actually, I could not take my eyes off his neck, because when he swallowed, his Adam's apple jumped up and down. His questions went stubbornly over the same topics, over and over, and were rather intrusive. He asked a lot about Charles and wrote down everything I said in his little black notebook. This made me feel oddly guilty, as if it all could be used against me at a later date.

Evidently, they have found a dead man in the harbour. At first, they thought he was a vagabond, but it was apparently Mick Flaherty. He had been badly beaten, but somebody was able to identify him. The cause of death was a knife-cut to his abdomen. The police insisted on giving me an exact description . . .

But yes, of course the news came as a shock to me. It was not long since he was here, full of life, speaking to me about his savings and how he would take the children with him to America. I don't know what happened afterwards. No-one tells me anything. Stead says that it is better that I should know nothing.

I leaf through the notes, back and forth. Annie Besant wrote sporadically and about all kinds of things. Sometimes, she was concerned about the garden and the endless rain that autumn or about her problems keeping servants. On one occasion – it was September 10 – someone threw a stone at the house, and it broke the pane in the front door window. Afterwards, she no longer dared to use that door. Apparently, Charles Leadbeater, and what he did to little boys, were the subjects of local rumours.

Now and then, the young policeman came back to the house, but he asked no further questions about Leadbeater, who had kept out of sight since August 9. It might be that the police were afraid that Annie would warn him that they were on his trail. In September, Leadbeater was already on his way to America in any case.

*

Again and again, Annie wrote about hearing noises in the night. She was afraid that someone might have got into the house.

20th September, 1905. The knocking started again just after 1 a.m. This time, I was determined not to let it pass and went downstairs to investigate. My heart was beating so hard I thought it would burst, and I was staggering rather than walking. I am alone in the house now that Cook has handed in her notice, and the Theosophists, who are unsure about me, are keeping their distance.

Naturally, there was no-one in Helena's room. I checked it carefully, shining a light along the skirting boards and testing all the window fastenings. Everything seemed secure, and no-one had touched the papers on her desk. I had deliberately left them in a certain disorder which had not been tampered with. The stove was cold, and the ashes cleaned out. But then, what had I expected?

Having searched her bedroom meticulously, I climbed the stairs to the attic. I did this even though I knew that it was insane to go there in the middle of the night. For one thing, someone in the street might see a light moving and raise the alarm. I actually believe that the police are keeping a round-the-clock watch on the house. Being found wandering around the attic at night would not improve my situation, but I felt I had no choice.

There was nothing much to see. Burrows must have cleared away most of the odds and ends, including his cameras and other pieces of equipment, before he himself disappeared – God alone knows where to. Some worn children's clothes were lying about, and I put them away tidily in the wooden box I had already used for the books Dora and Thomas had brought. That tin ship Stead once gave the little lad also went into the box. Why should anyone find the toy and wonder about it? There was a sharp smell in the air up there due to spilt chemicals, particularly in the cubby-hole they used as a darkroom. I must remember to clean it thoroughly. Meanwhile, I pulled quite a few things in front of the darkroom door. It is small and hard to notice, unless one is looking for it.

The persistent police officer, who is called Charles Trump, was less than helpful when I asked for protection. I feel increasingly that the house is no longer safe, and I am of a mind to leave. As a matter of fact, the Keightleys have written to suggest that very thing. I have heard nothing from Charles, but William calls now and then. He is very kind and obviously worried. All that we have worked for has been endangered, and no-one will pay the slightest attention to anything we say.

Herbert Burrows really has disappeared without a trace. William has not heard from him for weeks, and his studio is apparently locked. His assistant, Jacob Hall, is also gone. Can the two of them have been doing something wrong?

Sometimes, I feel as if I were under siege. I cannot help remembering dear Miss Clark and her stories about Lucknow. Worse, I begin to think of this house as my grave, and it frightens me a great deal.

At this point, there is a break in Annie's notes. She takes them up again on September 28. Officer Trump is back in the house, and I feel they may have talked together in this room. Annie recorded their conversation verbatim.

Trump was here again this morning. By now, he hardly even tries to be polite. He really is a very unpleasant young man, but the news he brought was truly terrible. He began by asking if I knew a certain Herbert Burrows, a photographer. Since Herbert's pictures have been used to illustrate several of my articles, there was no point in denying that I did. Trump wrote down my answer apparently word for word, but stared rudely at me the entire time.

"When did you last see Mr Burrows?" he asked.

"I cannot tell you exactly. At the beginning of August, I think. He did a great deal of work here, taking photographs of our sessions."

"And you haven't seen him since?"

"No."

"Mrs Besant, I want you to take a good look at this."

Trump produced a bundle wrapped in sailcloth and tied with

rope. He unfolded its contents slowly to show me something looking like a dirty blanket.

"It's a man's coat. It got torn where it was ripped by a pole on the way down, as it were. Do you recognise it?"

The woollen material gave off a stale smell of something rotting, the way leaf-mould smells or, better, leaves cleared from the bottom of the fountain in late autumn.

"No, I have no memory of seeing this before."

"Mrs Besant, it's highly likely that this coat belonged to Herbert Burrows. You see, we believe it's his body we found at one of the construction sites at Victoria Station. Unfortunately, the corpse's face had been mostly eaten away by rats and eels."

He went on to explain that workmen had seen the corpse float to the surface, the area having been badly undermined by rain. Apparently, the coat had a nametag with Burrows's name, so it seemed a reasonable assumption that the body was his. It had got stuck under the water among some tough old roots.

Trump waited to see what impact his words would have on me. I felt the bile rise to my mouth and forced myself to swallow. I could think of nothing to say. Trump cleared his throat, and his Adam's apple bounced up and down, but this time he did not seem hesitant.

"Mrs Besant, we have reason to believe that Burrows was involved in an illegal child-prostitution racket. He may in fact have been a kind of pimp. We also believe that in these matters he collaborated with Charles Leadbeater, as well as one or several other persons."

Trump spoke more loudly as he came to the end of his sentence. It sounded as if he was losing control and perhaps saying more than he should. The sour taste returned to my mouth, and I had to spit into my handkerchief. All the time, Trump was staring at me. His eyes looked so very unpleasant. So pale and expressionless. The coat was lying on the floor, unrolled and spreading its disgusting smell of mud and rot, somehow intensified by the warmth of the room.

Looking at it properly, one could see that it had once been of good quality, though the cloth was badly soiled. It had well-cut lapels and shiny buttons. I found myself wondering if the coat had been given to the man in part-payment or maybe had been bought with his savings.

Also, I wondered if Burrows could handle a knife. Maybe I had known all the time. Well, in a general way at least.

That very moment, the knocking resumed, louder and more distinct then ever before. Detective Trump started, making me feel relieved that he too could hear it. I normally didn't hear it during the day, at least not in daylight.

"I thought you were alone in the house!"

He brusquely pushed past me to run downstairs. His footfalls echoed through the house, making me think of Flaherty and the way he had run past me and down the stairs that evening. He had found his way up to the attic without anyone noticing. Up there, he had seen something that had upset him very, very badly. Something terrible. William told me about this later on.

Presumably, Trump believed that I was hiding Charles in the basement, or maybe kept Dora locked into some dark cupboard. This made me almost want to laugh, recognising how stupid he was after all. All his cunning questions and fierce staring had been alarming, but when I heard him slamming doors and thumping about I felt I knew him better. Of course, he found nothing at all.

Gupta is sitting on a cardboard box, his feet in leather slippers dangling just above the floor. He looks hot in his sweater. The room is very warm and the air heavy to breathe, even though the sun has not yet worked its way round to the back of the house. The dry, stuffy smell in here makes me feel that in some inexplicable way, the hot summer of ninety-odd years ago is still lodged in the walls. I long for something to drink.

"This ends on September 28 – nothing more from 1905. Didn't

she write anything else?" I have the impression that my voice is being absorbed into the hot air.

"No. Well, not directly."

"Indirectly?"

"Some of her correspondence with Alice Frobisher is still kept in our main archive. It is not that interesting. They found Dora in a house in Poplars after one year. Annie Besant and William Stead had been looking for the girl all that time. Stead went round the workhouses and hostels, asking everyone he met about her. When he found her, Dora had already stopped talking. There was a doctor's certificate that she was psychologically unstable." He makes a face.

"The word *idiot* was apparently used. The boy, Tom, was never found." Gupta looks regretful.

I leaf through the document folder again and find the Blavatsky photographs at the back. The portraits by Herbert Burrows are well preserved, but the snap from the ferry has gone quite black. The image of Helena Blavatsky kept changing until she could no longer be seen.

The Clay People

KIM RESPONDS AS soon as I press the door-phone button at Howell & Peters. Getting the door open is easy, but I have to push my way past five young suits, their faces riddled with acne, presumably on their way out to lunch. They move like an army unit, shoulder to shoulder. My shoulder is hurting, and I'm still furious when I get into the lift. It has always baffled me how anyone could feel young men were the slightest bit cuddly. The lift mirror presents me with a dull, greenish version of myself looking grim, with greasy hair and the lines round my eyes picked out by the bright light. On a good day – if I were younger or if someone were kind – my wrinkles might be called laugh lines. Instead, I believe I've acquired them by screwing up my eyes when I stare into the distance after people who've left me. My jacket has obviously been around for twenty years if a day, even though I've only worn it for five. It has known previous owners whose smells still emerge like ghostly presences from the coarse tweed, especially when it's warm or rainy.

On the phone, Kim didn't want to say what she and Neil had found, but insisted that I'd be interested. When pressed, she admitted to an old newspaper headline about "clay people". I haven't a clue what that means. The lift goes down and down. To pass the time, I push a few strands of my hair over to the left. Not a great change from the right, but different at least. Finally, the grey doors part with a whoosh.

I'm back inside the submarine. On the way to Kim's room, I pass a series of notices fastened to the white concrete wall, ordering appropriate behaviour. NO SMOKING. NO DRINKING. No heavy breathing . . . OK, that's my own addition. I need to calm down, my heart is beating wildly, and there is Kim Darken, waiting for me in the doorway. She is dressed in something glowing and bottle green, as usual, but her hair is even redder and more voluminous than I remember. She looks like one of the women painted by Dante Gabriel Rossetti, like a Beatrice of heavenly beauty.

"We've found something fucking amazing!" she calls out when I'm still 10 yards away.

I wave at her, mainly to show that I've heard her. Because I've got my father's liver-coloured briefcase squeezed under one arm, I feel a little like Daddy on his way home from work. Maybe it's just my smelly tweed jacket that makes my thoughts wander like this. In the briefcase are the Blavatsky photographs, which I've brought along with the intention of asking if anyone at H&P reads Russian.

Neil is sitting at his computer, as ever, and his face is still as pale as ever. Today he actually looks interested. Kim carries on talking as she follows me, saying that she and Neil have been working all week on the 1930s and, quite coincidentally, came across something that had to do with my story. She pushes me towards a table where a few brittle old newspapers have been spread out. There are copies of papers from a police investigation too, and photographs. The policeman was called Chief Superintendent Charles Edgar Trump. The investigation date was 1939.

I lean forward to examine the photographs. The detail is almost perfect.

The photos show a row of half-naked children softly bedded down in mud.

*

It is a truly unbelievable story. Kim points me in the direction of the background articles, all of which begin by describing a new idea for a central-heating system.

During the winter of 1938, civil servants working for a company set up by the Pimlico Local Authority and called the District Heating Undertaking decided to utilise the presence of the large, newly built Battersea Power Station, located on the river-bank immediately opposite the planned council housing estate at (?) Garden [the estate had not yet been named] on the "city-side". The great power station was seen as a symbol of a new era, the start of the half-century as yet ten years away. In January 1938, the ten members of the Heating Undertaking's Board resented their plan to lead heated water from specially constructed turbines in the power station through under-river tunnels into a water tank placed at a height of 125 feet, to be located on the site of the estate. The hot water would be conducted from there to the taps and modern hot-water radiators in individual homes.

The cooled water would be re-circulated back to Battersea though massive, large-bore pipes. Technically complex, this daring project strengthened the British sense of national confidence at a time when the threat of war from a fully armed and Nazi-ruled Germany was becoming ever more likely.

As soon as the worst of the winter cold had passed, digging started on the south bank of the river. It took until the beginning of August 1939, the end of a very hot and dry summer beating more than thirty-year-old London record, before the start of the main excavation of the clay to the west of the tracks entering Victoria Station. On August 15th, workmen encountered a chest with macabre, to say the least, contents.

The cuttings include an eyewitness account, as told to a reporter from the *Daily Mail*.

CLAY PEOPLE

London, August 16th, 1939.

During the early hours of yesterday morning, an unusual and macabre find was made near the river at Victoria Station. The site is currently being excavated in order to lay the pipe-work for the new district heating installation linked to Battersea Power Station. Mr Alfred Siddock, foreman for Barclays' Dredging and Construction Ltd, made the terrifying discovery.

Mr Siddock told our reporter: "I had just started off our dredgers. We were a team of eight men with the job of breaking up the clay as best we could. We had to work our way down step by step, building wooden walls round the hole as we went along to prevent mudslides. We'd got down some 30 feet or so when one of the men started shouting 'For Christ's sake, stop your pickaxes! There's something here!'

"It took us the best part of an hour to free the thing. It was a chest, looking like an old tin trunk of the kind you might stick live fish in to keep them fresh, with a row of holes drilled all round it. Having said that, the smell it gave off was far from fresh. It was as stale as if from an old bog. Charlie [Bicks] and I set to breaking the lid open and hose the mud inside away. Charlie was holding the hose, but he dropped it when he saw what was inside. It was several almost naked, dead children. I've ***ing well never seen anything like it, though I've been working by the river for twenty years!"

Later, our reporter learned that the bodies have been taken by boat to the police mortuary in the eastern harbour area. Further investigations will be carried out under the supervision of Chief Superintendent C. E. Trump. At present, the Chief Superintendent does not wish to comment other than to say that some old unsolved crime may well be the explanation of this macabre find.

The article is illustrated with a poor-quality shot showing the site where the chest was found. It's impossible to see more than walls of clay and the hollow where the chest had been, with a clumsy white cross marking the spot. It looks like a wartime image, maybe from the bog-like trenches in the First World War. I suppose the boys would have ended up in one of those trenches if they hadn't died so young. A small oval photo of the Chief Superintendent inserted in a corner shows a middle-aged face with fatty ridges and rough skin. He could be anyone.

Close to me, Kim is leaning forward over the table.

"The cold-store of the mortuary was hit by a German bomb in November 1940, but by then the boys had been pretty carefully investigated, at least by the standards of the day. Trump will have drawn his conclusions. It seems he'd been working on the case since 1905 and was unwilling to let it go. He must have been convinced that he'd found the murder victims this time. The photographs do tell a story, don't they?"

The children's bodies were remarkably well preserved. The mud seems to have excluded air almost entirely from the chest, and their skin, nails and hair look almost as if they were still alive. It is as if they had been kept in a sealed time capsule. They are lying there, with their mouths closed and eyes tightly shut, as if wanting to keep out the unaccustomed daylight for a little longer. Were it not for the quick-drying, rough surface of the clay, lending the same dark grey shade to eyes, eyebrows and hair, they might just have fallen asleep for a while. There are five boys, about nine or ten years of age.

"Did Trump write a report?"

"Yes, and it was quite exhaustive. It had private notes all over it. He didn't have the time to delete them. It begins with medical data."

Kim starts to read aloud from her notes.

"Several of the boys had bruises round their necks, presumably due to a noose, but the cause of death was not strangulation. Rather, it seems they were poisoned. Their stomachs contained mescaline in fatal doses. The analysis wasn't that sophisticated, but their stomach contents were remarkably intact. Also, one boy was different from the rest. That one there, number 5." She points to one of the close-ups.

The boy, like the other children, has only got on a pair of thin cotton shorts. His hair is thick and quite long, his eyebrows straight and a little raised, making him look surprised. His eyelids are not quite shut, and bending over the picture I can see a hint of dark under his eyelashes. The thin membrane of clay over his face is so dry it's about to crack, the fracture lines forming a network like the fissures in a dry riverbed.

For a brief moment, I fear that the boy's eyes will open and he will see us.

Tapping on the picture with her nail, Kim says, "His mouth was full of leaves with toothmarks in them. He must have chewed them, so they weren't put there after death. Trump was very upset by this, writes that this is 'conclusive evidence', but never explains exactly what he's referring to. You see, he had no time. He was killed in the Blitz, just outside the entrance to Aldgate Tube station and only a few nights before the mortuary was hit. But the leaves were identified. They came from foxglove plants. *Digitalis* something. It grows all over the place."

*

Trump's report, or at least parts of it, is there among the other material. During the war, Howell & Peters's archives swallowed it up as a complement to the pictures, and Neil has located it. Trump's handwriting is cramped, tight with small loops, and he left very little space between the lines as if he was short of space.

Neil has ambled over to join us now, trying not to seem too interested. He has twisted his monitor screen round to get up from his desk, and I see what he's been up to.

A small hazy staircase leads up into the country called MYST.

"May I borrow this?" I ask, holding up Trump's report. Kim nods, and Neil says nothing. "By the way, does anyone round here read Russian?" I hold out the blackened photo.

Neil grabs it. Golly, a man of many parts.

"*Lotjsij katjstvo*. 'The best quality'. What's this about?"

"Breaking the Trades Descriptions Act," I tell him.

Correspondence

L ETTER FROM CHARLES Edgar Trump to Father Martin Sander, Dundalk, Ireland. The date was August 24, 1939. The carbon copy was registered by H&P in February 1941.

Dear Friend,

I assume that you by now have had the time to go through the newspaper cuttings I sent you. Indeed, this is a truly awful story, but there is no harm in casting some light over these events of long ago, in order to clarify what actually took place. Perhaps this is particularly valuable now that we are once more on the brink of war.

You surely recall, as well as I do, the impossible circumstances under which my investigation laboured at the outset. Now that most of those originally involved are dead, the truth about Charles Leadbeater must be told.

As you may also remember, one of your ex-parishioners, a man called Michael Flaherty, of Galway, latterly of Dundalk, was murdered and that I was assigned to investigate the case. It turned out to be part of a criminal set-up with perverse and possibly also occult features. Your help in these matters was invaluable to me, and so I feel not the slightest hesitation about breaking the rules of police secrecy. This time, at least, the ends must justify the means. So – let me go back in time to "my first case" in 1905.

We had a letter from an anonymous informer in connection with the discovery of Michael Flaherty's body (it had been dumped at a dockside brewery). I later suspected a young Swedish photographer, Jacob Hall, who was a member of the circle round Annie Besant and Charles Leadbeater. Later still, I became convinced that Hall was our informant. He shared Hampstead lodgings with another young man called Albert Blair, and for various reasons I kept a close watch on him. Still, he might have been relatively harmless, and I had no reason to go after a young lad who finally decided to confess. A few years later, he showed the good sense to go to the United States. Blair fell in the Battle of the Somme in 1916, taking any knowledge or guilt with him.

Now, as you know, Hall's claim was that an indecent, unnatural traffic in little children was taking place. Orphaned slum children were being picked up and prostituted, a business that was very profitable. The key man, or at least one of the key men, was Pastor Charles Leadbeater, active as a "fire-and-brimstone" preacher in London's Theosophical Society. Leadbeater selected his victims himself, under the guise of a philanthropic wish to "give children a better chance in life". This was quite untrue. As a sideline, he also seems to have carried out some kind of "research" on the boys. We did get Leadbeater, but not until a year later, when he was prac-tising his old trade in Chicago. That set of events was well described in The Illustrated Police News, *so I need not dwell on it. However, we got nowhere with regard to the London crimes. Leadbeater admitted nothing, even though we kept him locked up for weeks. We simply had no proof that he had harmed anyone. Not until now, when the bodies of these boys speak their own incontrovertible language.*

Let me add just one more detail. After a careful site investiga-tion, we were sure that the chest had been moved quite a distance from its original burial place. I gather that a stream feeding the river ran through the area, and that whatever was in the clay carried on flowing along the original ravine, down towards the Thames and the old marshland. Not that this was of any particu-lar significance to our work, but it is a remarkable phenomenon!

Anyway, the tangled mess in London got sorted out in the end, and some of the middlemen were properly sentenced. Apart from a handful of Soho street traders, there was a Russian chap who copied the lewd photos and used his Charing Cross Station shop as an outlet and centre for making contacts. Sadly, we never got a handle on either the organisers or the customers. Those characters cared for nothing or nobody except themselves and all used aliases, usually from the world of the West End theatre, where most of them operated. The list of clients was said to include members of the higher echelons, including Cabinet Ministers, but proving it was impossible. For one thing, it would have been interpreted as anti-government propaganda dreamt up by anarchists, some of the more hysterical Suffragettes or a variety of other crackpots. Be that as it may, we were given explicit orders to focus on the circle round Leadbeater. I must say that William Stead, the newspaperman and good friend of Annie Besant, was high on my list of suspects, but he went down with the Titanic, of course.

Well, we smoked out the vipers' nest anyway. Many of these homosexuals and paedophiles jumped ship in a panic and fled to the Continent, so some good came out of it. It was rather like the aftermath of the Wilde affair. Good riddance, I say! If they hadn't decamped, I have no doubt that ordinary decent people would have gone all out to settle old scores. It is of course not difficult to spot who these "gentlemen" are, since their weak characters and effeminate manners usually give them away pretty quickly. As far as I am concerned, all the perverts of this ilk have got but one goal in mind, and that is to undermine public order and the values of Christian family life. I will say this for myself, I have made it a personal goal to cleanse society of as much of this filth as possible. Trying to "understand" and therefore tolerate these people will only give the tumour room to spread. Then where would we be?

However, my dear friend, I am letting my feelings run away with me. I shall do my very best to provide little Thomas Flaherty with a decent homecoming so that he will rest in consecrated ground next to his mother. There is no doubt in my own mind that I have really found him.

Another detail: he was holding a little key in his hand, one of those things used to wind up mechanical toys. I've still got it.

Having said all this, it is of some concern to me that several witnesses, including William Stead and Annie Besant, claim to have seen *the boy* with their own eyes after the burial in 1905 and also in 1906, though admittedly never close enough to speak to him. Another curious circumstance is that the boy had the same kind of half-chewed leaves in his mouth as did his father. I feel I am straying into your area of expertise here, worrying about the peace of the soul and unhappy spirits. Well, there is certainly "more between Heaven and Earth" than we mortals can fathom! Do you have any theories?

With my best wishes,
Charles

Letter from Father Martin Sander, Dundalk, Ireland, to Chief Super-intendent Charles Edgar Trump, London WC2. The date was September 15, 1939.

Registered by H&P in February 1941.

My dear friend,

It was indeed a startling coincidence that I should receive the letter from you so soon after the past had surfaced again, as it were. Finding the dead boys was a truly dreadful business, but at the same time a relief. I would like to go to London, maybe some time next year, if the investigation of the bodies is delayed by this new war. It may sound lugubrious, but I would very much like to see the objects that were found for myself – that is, the chest and the few things found buried with the boys.

About two years ago, I had a visit from a Mrs Alice Frobisher and a young friend or ward of hers, Miss Myrtle Black. I am sure you remember that the name Frobisher turned up in our investigations once, even though it was so long ago – all of thirty-four years! I must say that the fate of little Dora made me deeply suspicious of the Frobishers, and I was prepared to deal with the woman firmly when we met. However, meeting her changed my mind. She was handsome, engaging and very frank. Only native caution prevented me from admitting that I had myself in any way been involved in attempting to clarify the circumstances of Michael Flaherty's death.

I do remember it all perfectly. I was only a young man at the time, the hard-worked 25-year-old curate to Father Keegan, who tended to be "tired and emotional" a lot of the time. I do believe that what you experience when you are young is what stays with you most vividly for the rest of your life.

Alice Frobisher asked me about the Flahertys, and I think it is fair to say that I handled her enquiry quite skilfully. I took her to see the grave, of course, and then showed her some old newspaper cuttings from Father Keegan's collection. Neither Mrs Besant nor the fact that her divorced husband, Frank Besant, and I are distant relatives was mentioned. Frank is a decent, good man, I must say, even though we do not agree about the teachings of the Church.

I hinted to Mrs Frobisher that the Flahertys were less than highly regarded locally, which is at least more true than not. In the circumstances, I suppose it might be accepted as a white lie. Flaherty was a dangerous man and, in these parts, a natural leader given that he was descended from one of the old families. People round here really believed not only that he was related to the old kings of Ireland but that he was a magician! It was not least the attitude of the Irish towards us English during the last war, when many made common cause with the enemy out of sheer hatred for us, that convinced me that I did the right thing when I sowed the rumour that Flaherty had gone mad, killing first his children and then himself. People here could not tolerate this, not even from a "King", and hardly a soul came to the funeral. Many were actually protesting that he should not have been buried in sacred soil, so it can truly be said that my untruth served its purpose.

Still, I did distort the truth and have always felt unhappy about the fate of these unhappy children. I tell myself that Flaherty would have been even more dangerous dead than alive – yet another Irish martyr slain by the English!

Instead, his name is never mentioned. Somebody set fire to his house a few years later. It was a pretty well ruined wee cottage anyway, but the story went round that Flaherty was walking again up there. Flickering lights had been seen, and dark shapes moving about. The belief is still widely held. Alice Frobisher naturally got nowhere at all with her questions. The villagers are incredibly superstitious.

Mentioning this reminds me of your question. I know you have asked me before, but I did not know then what I do now. These leaves you found come from Digitalis purpura, or common purple foxglove. It has been believed for a very long time that the leaves confer eternal life . . .

August 30, 1998

A S D F G . . . DAMN, THE D F G keys get stuck in a frenzied metallic cluster. I try to sort it. The typewriter is an old Continental 340, manufactured somewhere in Germany called Siegmarschönau, and smells of old machine-oil and dust. Jacob bought it in Berlin between the wars, after seeing Leni Riefenstahl's film *Triumph of the Will* in a Kurfürstendamm cinema. He admired the film a great deal, and it was at this time that he started writing texts about his photographs, profound but often contradictory articles. Unlike the current media clichés about the sufficiency of the image, he thought visual records were not enough, because situations were normally too complex for a photograph to catch more than a small fraction of the truth.

I'm installed at the large dining table in Jacob's sitting room – well, my sitting room now – and the rain is pouring down outside. The little plot of grass in the yard is completely sodden, and the branches of the large horse chestnut tree already seem weighed down with a kind of autumnal darkness. Sweeping slowly in the wind, dripping with wet, each branch threatens to let loose a shower of spiky little fruits. When I open the window, I can hear the tree swooping, whispering, slapping with its five-fingered leaf-hands. The leaves bend inwards like tobacco leaves about to turn into long Havana cigars.

The Birdman isn't around today. Presumably, he doesn't care to go out in this rain with his little bag of breadcrumbs. He is a modest, small being in a grey hat and black coat worn regardless of the season. He grew up in Danzig, and sometimes we try to speak in German, hesitantly, using plain, childish rows of words without syntax. Now and then, I watch him from the kitchen window when he sneaks into the old Jewish cemetery. He finds his way between the gravestones, his head turning like a worried fieldmouse sniffing the wind for danger, in order to put stones on the graves. His anonymous gifts, warmed by his hands, are put in different places each time. Since he cannot possibly be related to all these people, I assume that his movements are part of a private ritual. Maybe it is a kind of sacrifice, maybe a cry in the wilderness. I have no idea.

My oily hands feel rough and smooth at the same time from picking up old grit worked into typewriter's greased crevices. I saw Jacob write on it so often. I remember his rather large hands with their prominent veins tapping away. My duster is removing even his fingerprints now. Z X C V . . . The less-used keys move more freely and don't show that tendency to lock like pointy teeth in an overcrowded jaw.

*

Four months have passed since I left England. I have had time to think and to accept that it is impossible to find answers to every question. Some facts make no sense in any context. It's like having sorted two jigsaw puzzles found in the attic all mixed together in the same old box of sweet-smelling cardboard. There will be pieces that just don't fit, and to expect otherwise would be silly.

I stayed on with P. V. Gupta for one more month. He kept padding about looking anxious, presumably because he was frightened that the police would come back. In fact, we never heard from them again.

By chance, I met the black slug-man, Al the policeman, in Howell & Peters one afternoon. He told me about finding this dead guy near Westbourne Grove in Notting Hill, "a skinhead, just a kid really, he'd been knifed in the belly. It was bad. Can't think how he got that far, but I guess he didn't realise how serious it was – you know, like when some people lose half a leg and just keep on going." Al postured for a bit; I think the idea was to show what a mover he was, and I slipped away before he got round to asking me along for some honky-tonk that weekend. The police say that they haven't identified the dead man, and they haven't found an injured woman either. It seems that "cunt" is anyway a term of general abuse – like "faggot" or "whore" or whatever. Six-year-olds now use these words in the playground. If "cunt" can mean anything that gets in your way, like a car or dog or fellow human being of any age or sex, it has become a new word, with its own secret hoard of meaning though defined by traditional values – like the coded words in the secret languages Jacob Hall loved so much.

*

The wind is blowing more strongly now, and I get up to close the window. Jacob must have left it half-open often, because the sill is as soft and porous as a sponge. I observe some people moving about in the yard. The handsome man from the second floor is gently manoeuvring an old bike between the puddles. The saddle is dark with soaked-up water. The man's hair is almost white, and he moves like an angel, lightly and gracefully. Even after closing the window, I can hear the tram passing. It's a humming, grinding noise that somehow travels easily through the glass. The sound is becoming familiar. I've spoken to a lot of people, not just the Birdman and the Angel but also a girl who lives across the landing. She is in her 20s and called Mia. All we've said is hello, but at least in my case these exchanges have meant real self-discipline. She knows what I look like now, and my name is there to read on my door.

*

I'm working on a big project. It will take a long time. I record graves about to be dismantled and got rid of. I wonder what happens to the stones. Crushed to gravel or construction rubble? They used to integrate old gravestones into walls, which helped to keep memories alive. It is not just the biographical details that interest me, but the choice of stone, the position of the grave and details like symbols of death. One common symbol is two pale hands clasping one another. Some stones have birds or weeping angels. Whenever the rain stops, I'm out and about, driving round to cemeteries and spending hours there. I'm sometimes approached, usually by some busybody, a bloke red-faced with pomposity, who wants to know what I think I'm doing. He has seen me writing and measuring and crawling about in the wet grass with my camera, taking note of things that are scheduled to be removed in the name of public order. It's not done to try to remember everything.

But most of the time I'm left in peace. I like the aromatic, lightly sedative scent of thujas in churchyards. I like the silence too. Sometimes I feel that, like the Birdman, I should leave a small stone on the graves I photograph. As a sign of gratitude or a memento, to show that I've been there.

*

Sander's letter was unfinished. Maybe Trump had taken the last pages with him that night when the bomb fell on Aldgate Tube station. Maybe he had in mind to search the bodies one more time when his own death intervened, though sometimes I wonder if a mere acci-dental detail like being killed actually stops you if you really want to do something. There must be things that you simply do anyway.

I was talking to an old mate of mine the other day. Well, we shared a friend, Peter and I: the photographer who was killed in Bosnia a few years ago. Peter was saying that the dead man's things are still in his lab because he's expected to come back home. At least in Peter's case, emotion won hands down over common sense.

Death cannot be understood. Though it might at times be possible to take pictures of it.

*

I have finally managed to interpret most of Jacob's notes. During the last years of his stay in London, he kept a diary of sorts, with un-annotated times for appointments and very brief comments. He must have stayed there until the end of March 1911, when he boarded a ship for America. During that time, he worked in a photographic studio at 63a, Baker Street, by Portman Square. The studio was called Window & Grove, and it had a smart black frame in Art Nouveau style surrounding the motto *Ars et Veritas*. Art and Truth. I found their advertisement among Jacob's papers. It is laid out like the two of hearts and shows two women embracing. I know nothing else about the studio, except that the boss was an American woman called Kay Mortimer. In Jacob's notes, she was KM and, later, Kay.

He hardly did anything that might have attracted attention. Occasionally, he went to a party or a play. He walked in Kew Gardens or along the river at Richmond. He met Albert quite often, but they no longer shared lodgings. After the Leadbeater scandal, Londoners were much less tolerant of queers. In 1906, the British public couldn't distinguish between homosexuality and paedophilia.

Jacob Hall became a more and more skilful photographer during his years in London, more than good enough for jobs in the United States. If he saw somebody special regularly, he did not keep notes about it. It might be that he thought it unwise. Still, Edwardian London was in many ways the last period of innocence, before two devastating world wars and the Spanish flu changed everything.

As always, thinking about the wars is enough to make me wonder how anyone could ever speak of them as natural after seeing how easily human beings can turn themselves into mud-and-blood soup. Or, to put it another way, how short is human memory really?

*

I light the gas to make a cup of tea and burn myself on the match, as usual. There must be a gas leak somewhere in the house, because the ring of flames always glows unevenly and erratically. On the kitchen table, today's paper is still open to a fascinating article I was reading this morning. Nine young sailors are to be dug up from the Svalbard permafrost. They all died of Spanish flu in 1918. The idea is to try to isolate the virus and understand the causes and effects of the infection better. Maybe it will be possible to revive the 80-year-old pathogen if it's still present in their tissues.

I had a card from Kim Darken the other day. She had been to see P. V. Gupta. He is still there, but the house at Lansdowne Road is due to be "refurbished within the month". The cat disappeared without a trace soon after I left, and this news made me feel improbably sad. The old home of the Theosophists is under new ownership. A consortium has bought it and is planning to make the building into a Centre for Information and Management Studies. I assume this will finally banish Helena Blavatsky and Annie Besant from the dark rooms.

Kim says that she is coming to Gothenburg to attend a photography fair and asks if she might stay with me for a couple of nights. I haven't answered her yet.

*

I pour the hot water over the tea leaves in the strainer and watch them float to the surface in a random pattern. Removing the strainer, I spoon in some honey and dilute the liquid with milk until it is a very pale brown. I watch the Angel through the window. He is walking across Frigga Street with one of his pale children riding on his shoulders. The child's small hands are held securely in his father's big ones. The rain has almost drifted away. I can hear the little boy's high-pitched, happy voice above the rumbling of the traffic.

*

I have carefully put a clean, complete copy of Jacob's papers in my Dad's briefcase and stored it in a safe, dry place. It is true, though, that you can never learn, or even remember, everything.

Epilogue

THIS IS AN imaginary story, even though I have made use of certain historical personalities, events and facts. Much of what I describe really happened, only not exactly as I say it did. The times are correct. For instance, the notorious Mme Blavatsky really did arrive in London in 1887. The Theosophist Annie Besant really was deeply engaged in the women's movement, as was the legendary newspaperman William Thomas Stead. By the way, Stead was a much more attractive personality than the man I have described. It is said, among other things, that he entertained his desperate fellow travellers on the *Titanic* with jokes and stories until the very last. Charles Leadbeater is a historical figure too and was as surrounded by scandal as he is in my narrative.

Number 17, Lansdowne Road was one of the London addresses at which Mme Blavatsky stayed. I took the liberty of picking a location near the wealthy area of Holland Park, but admit that a glance at the map of London shows that there are nearly twenty streets with the same name.

– E.-M.L.